Dusk Walking

The first book of the trilogy

by

ZOE QUINN SHAW

Copyright © 2012 Zoe Quinn Shaw
All rights reserved.
ISBN: 1475275250
ISBN-13: 978-1475275254

THIS BOOK IS DEDICATED TO MY FRIENDS AND FAMILY.

ACKNOWLEDGMENTS

This novel has been four years of my life, so I have many people to thank for taking part in the creation of *Dusk Walking*. I would like to thank those listed with all of my heart.

Steven Shaw

Joyce Narvades

Isabel Shaw

Jess Frey

Lyne Belleau

Eliza Clarke

Claire Wagler

Sara Johnston

Carlo N. Samson

Friends have come and gone over the years, and some of those friends helped build *Dusk Walking* even more than the ones listed above. We may have moved on, but I will not forget what they did for this story.

CHAPTER ONE

Jack locked his seatbelt into place and honked the horn once, twice, then three times in hopes of leading Luke away from the other Dusk Walkers. Unfortunately, he succeeded. In the rearview mirror, Jack spotted the Hunter running through the park to catch up with the car, and he veered off the path onto the uneven terrain of the grass. The stunt would add yet another crime to the long record of trouble that he had caused, but he had lost the ability to care a long time ago. The Dusk Walkers were, after all, only in the park to have some fun, regardless of the rules about driving through it.

He drove in reverse over flowerbeds and past fences, backing into swing sets and benches until he found a place to turn around. Ahead of him, Luke's flashlight approached. The event that had given all of them powers had made the Hunters blind in the dark and the Dusk Walkers intolerant to sunlight.

He arrived near the top of a slope and slammed his foot onto the brakes, thrusting him backward into his seat and then forward into the steering wheel. His seatbelt locked in place so that he did not break his nose, but the belt's tightness left him short of breath for several seconds.

Slowly, when he was able to breathe, Jack lifted his head and gasped. Luke was on his way, racing toward him faster than even the most powerful car could drive. Jack steered so that he would drive forward, then floored the gas. Cringing every time he almost hit a tree, he made it his next goal to return to the path. It was not big enough to accommodate the car, but it was better than the trees.

He skidded straight through a fence and back onto the gravel, driving as fast as he could down the path. His eyes were peeled open so wide that he thought they would fall out at any second. He turned the headlights back on.

When he was certain that Luke no longer followed him, Jack lost control of the car. The engine puttered to a stop, the steering wheel turned on its own, and everything that he could see shut down, apart from the headlights. He looked ahead and saw none other than Gianna, the second Hunter, who could control technology without lifting a finger. His heartbeat accelerating, he could only watch her while she stood in front of him, the dusty glow of the headlights illuminating her leather jacket, blue jeans, and sleek brown hair. He could not see her eyes, which were hidden by glasses that reflected the light.

"Driving without a license, are we?" Gianna's arm moved at her side, and at the end of it was her police-issued gun. Jack swallowed hard.

His seatbelt released when he had not touched it, and the driver-side door swung open.

"Step out of the car and put your hands in the air."

On foot, she was not fast enough to catch Jack.

Without any technology on him, he would be able to run away. It was for that reason that he pulled his bag onto his back and stepped out of the car with his hands raised above his head, his palms spread open.

Across the path, too close to the car to be a coincidence, a tree burst into flames. The fire burned the leaves to ashes and licked at the trunk until it was black. Knowing the most likely source of the flames, Jack backed away from Gianna instead of approaching her.

"Timberrrrr!" said a tiny voice not far from the tree, which crushed the car that he had just left and acted as a flaming barrier between Jack and Gianna.

He stumbled away from the fumes and whirled around, searching for a familiar face. When he did not find it, he cupped his hands around his mouth and called out, "Hey! Get to the bridge and find the others."

"Okay!" The youngest Dusk Walker, the fire-wielder, darted off, a shadow amongst the trees. Jack left in the opposite direction, hoping that Gianna would follow him instead of his friends. Alas, he had just told her where to find them.

He leapt over the fence and off of the path, putting as much distance between him and the Hunter as he could. The park was full of trees, but they were too thin to hide behind and too young to climb. He could only continue to search for the roads, but Central Park was a maze, especially in the dark. Jack had run so much that he had no idea where he was or where the four other Dusk Walkers were.

He paused to catch his breath and pressed the tips of his fingers into his side to settle the cramp there. When he was able to stand up straight, he turned on the spot, his ears open for any sound. There were a few distant shouts, then silence. Maybe everyone had forgotten about him. It wouldn't be the first time.

Jack spat out a curse when he saw the beam of a flashlight rapidly approaching him. He looked to his left and to his right, but there was nothing that could hide him. Tunnel vision kicking in, he had no choice but to dive behind the nearest bush. With all the luck in the world, he would not be spotted.

He pulled his knees to his chest and held his breath, keeping two eyes on the light as it came nearer. Judging by the amount of twigs and leaves that crunched underneath the Hunter's heavy steps, it was Luke. He slowed to a walk only yards behind Jack.

"Come out, come out, wherever you are…"

Jack shuddered. Luke was almost directly behind the bush, the flashlight's beam pointing straight ahead. When he could see the Hunter to his left, Jack's heart almost stopped. Luke, roughly ten years his senior, was only a few feet away from him. He was taller than Jack would ever be, handsomer too. His job, along with his two partners, was to find and capture the Dusk Walkers, who were legendary local terrorists. Whether or not the media invented half of their stories was unknown to everyone except to the Hunters and to the five children themselves.

A wolf's howl broke the silence. From what Jack could tell, it was somewhere toward the east. He smiled, recognizing another Dusk Walker's powers. Luke shined his flashlight toward the trees and abandoned his hide-and-seek game with Jack to chase the wolf.

He could breathe again. Jack made no quick movements when he climbed to his feet, making sure that the beam of light that accompanied Luke was gone before he stood. The Hunter would surely fail to catch the shape-shifting girl in the woods because she could turn into a bird and fly away.

With that idea to comfort him, he continued through the park, making as little noise as possible as he searched for the exit. Finally, past a playground with particularly noisy leaves under his feet, he heard sirens and the chatter of people. Usually that meant nothing good for him, but this time it was the only way he could return to base, where the other Dusk Walkers would be waiting for him.

Jack broke into a run when he saw the signs that led him in the right direction. He was so close. He could see the flashes of light between the trees, and he could hear the reporters shouting at each other to get the best possible shot of whoever would be the first to leave the park.

Just before he entered their line of sight, without any prior warning, he was tackled to the ground, his arm crushed underneath him. He spat out the dirt and dry leaves that had found their way into his mouth, and he searched for his attacker, but failed to find one. When he tried to sit up, a boot pushed him back down again. He watched the shoe gradually appear on his chest, followed by a long leg, black shorts, a fitted T-shirt, blond hair, and green night-vision goggles.

"Jack Turner, you're under arrest for vandalism, breaking and entering, etcetera," said the third and final Hunter, who was capable of becoming invisible at will. Rae dangled a pair of handcuffs above Jack's head. "Put these on."

"Aren't you supposed to read me my rights?" Jack took the handcuffs, but he did not put them on. Rae gave a heavy sigh.

"You have the right to remain silent. Anything you say or do can and will be held against you in a court of law. You have the right to an attorney. If you cannot afford an attorney, one will be provided for you. But I sincerely doubt any lawyer will want to help you, so good luck there. Do you understand the rights that I have just read you?"

Jack grumbled something so unintelligible that even he had no idea what he had said. Rae ignored him and lifted a walkie-talkie to her lips, not even asking him to repeat himself. While the radio gurgled, she removed her boot from his chest, and he bolted, leaving the handcuffs behind.

Usually, he only thought five seconds ahead and never had a plan to justify his spontaneous actions. This was still the case. He ran, doubting that he could get away without Rae eventually catching him, but that night he was lucky several times.

Before the youngest Hunter could catch him, he left the park and stumbled straight into a gathering of reporters and cameras. He reeled for only a moment, then shoved past a man who tried to talk to him, and he was free. Once on the street, Jack jogged down the sidewalk, pulled up his hood, and joined the crowd. He wedged himself between a girl with a giant handbag and a man wearing a black coat, then began to walk more swiftly. Walking would attract less attention, but he still needed to get farther away from the park.

Within minutes he was at a satisfactory distance from Central Park. He exhaled slowly as he walked, marveling at his escape, and when he was alone on the sidewalk he looked up at the cloudy, dark sky. Dusk had passed without him noticing. Night had completely fallen, and once he rejoined his friends, the real fun could begin.

CHAPTER TWO

A week after the incident in Central Park, Jack's shoelaces clicked against the subway tracks of District Three, the abandoned district of New York City. He tugged idly on his army dog tags. Ever since he had woken on the night of the unsolved power-plant meltdown, nicknamed the Explosion, the blank tags had always been around his neck. The smaller one had a chip in its corner that had been dulled down during the time he could not remember. The Dusk Walkers and the Hunters, the eight people affected by the Explosion, were still victims of amnesia towards their non-powered past, even three years after the incident.

He walked in a straight line, keeping a close eye on the third rail that looked so innocent, but raced with hundreds of volts of deadly electricity.

"Crap." His shoes squeaked as he lost his balance, and he almost fell onto the most dangerous rail. His heart rose to his throat, thumping wildly after his near-death. He straightened carefully, keeping his trembling arms outstretched for balance. He could have died. That would have been his demise: death by stumble. He stood for a moment and listened to his ragged breathing that echoed in the air. When he knew that he was not going to die, he chuckled nervously. His adrenaline pumped through his blood faster than a racecar, and the thrill sparked a feral grin on his lips.

He sucked in a deep breath and continued to walk along the tracks.

The city hated the Dusk Walkers, or at least they hated what they thought the Dusk Walkers were. The image projected of the children was that of five emaciated threats who presented a great danger to New York. The terror created by the Dusk Walkers was part of the reason why so few people had remained in the city and why hardly anyone moved in. There was also the Explosion. The radiation it had emitted was the cause of the deaths of millions of citizens. Millions more fled when the initial crisis was over. Tourists were a rarity in the Big Apple. The city divided into three districts after the effects of the Explosion had settled: The first belonged to the few businesses that still managed, the second was the home of most of the remaining civilians, and the third was deserted, being the area closest to the radiation and therefore still dangerous to a certain degree.

Jack hoisted himself onto the platform with great effort. It had been easier to climb onto the tracks than off. He hooked his foot onto the floor above and rolled onto the raised area. He walked for almost a minute through the empty station, his footsteps echoing off the walls. Past the dated poster of a Broadway play, he found the doorway that led to his friends.

He ducked under the old yellow police tape that fenced off the entrance to the passageway where the other Dusk Walkers slept. He blinked to adjust to the dim lighting and counted the four dormant bodies. They were all there.

"Everyone up, the sun just set," said Jack.

They had a busy night ahead of them. Their only allies in the city, the street gang known as the Nor'easters, were ready to make a deal with the Dusk Walkers. Jack and his friends needed more brute force behind them, whereas the Nor'easters wished to have the kids on their side to move the gang up the ladder of the underground hierarchy of New York. That night, they would finalize their contract.

Jack tapped his foot on the floor as Eva's blond head stirred first. Perhaps she was waking up, but she had most likely just turned in her sleep at his voice. They had fought for days about trusting the Nor'easters. He argued that the Dusk Walkers needed allies, and if it meant affiliating themselves with one of the midlevel street gangs of the city, so be it. They were lucky enough to not be chased away as they had been for years.

For example, not more than a day after the Explosion, he had made the mistake of demonstrating his powers in front of another person. The stranger had called some of his friends, who had assisted in leaving Jack beaten and bloody against the dumpster outside of a Brooklyn laundromat.

According to Eva, when she had woken up with no memories, she had gone straight to the hospital for help. Instead of finding the cure for her amnesia, the doctors had tried to make a lab rat out of her. She had luckily fought her way out.

All of the Dusk Walkers had a similar story from before they had found each other. The Hunters had been more fortunate. As soon as the five children had begun to raid the city at night, only months after the Explosion, the New York Police Department had assembled the three remaining people who had been affected by the radiation. Jack did not know the entire story. He only knew what he had seen with his own eyes and what he had read in the papers. The Hunters had undergone an intense training course over six months to prepare for work with the NYPD before they began to chase down the Dusk Walkers. Nonetheless, Jack and his friends were stubborn enough to stay inside the city. District Three was the perfect hiding place. The only problem was when they had to leave it to find food.

He cleared his throat. "Get up!" He nudged Cordy's leg, and she kicked at his foot. He leapt backward to avoid being harmed.

"Go screw yourself." She sat up in her nest of old clothes and glared at him. She began to run her fingers through Alix's curly hair to untangle the knots.

"Come on, guys, up and at 'em. We can finally leave this place tonight."

When the girls were all awake, Jack gathered his shabby blankets and rolled them tightly to fit them into his backpack. His bag mostly contained food and spare clothes, although there were other objects inside, such as a lock-pick, a map, pliers, a flashlight, and other practical objects stolen from stores. As for his own knife, he kept it in his belt for whenever he might need it. He had found it a year previously, abandoned on the side of the road.

Since then, it had been his. He shouldered his bag and watched as his friends finished packing.

They often called Cordy the Ghost-Whisperer. She could call upon the dead to spy for her or to warn her about approaching dangers. Despite her irritable nature, she had enough motherly care for all of them with some to spare. She was sixteen years old, according to the wanted posters.

Eva, who was the same age as Cordy, was amazing in fights against the Hunters, and she could sneak around places that they had to pass without being perceived. She had grace and agility that could only be imagined. Jack did not pay attention to how long his eyes lingered on her. When she lifted her hand to push a stray lock of hair behind her ear, she turned to look at him. He bit the inside of his cheek and turned away.

Lily was three years younger than Cordy and Eva. She could turn into different animals when she wanted, which came in handy in tight spots. On occasion, if it was more practical, she could even communicate with the creatures around her to learn about past events.

Young Alix's hair was still tangled, but it did not seem to bother her. She had simply tied it up with an elastic band. The ten-year-old used her fire powers more often during the cool October weather to keep the five of them warm. She still had trouble mastering her abilities, but it was becoming steadily easier for her as she practiced.

As for Jack, he could heal impossibly fast. Small cuts and burns took only seconds to heal, but as he had discovered a couple of years ago after a violent fall from a first-storey window, broken bones took several minutes before they completely healed. It had been a failed attempt to complete a shortcut, of which he preferred not to speak. He looked no older than fifteen, but in reality he was approaching his eighteenth birthday. He associated the slow aging process with his healing ability.

"All right," he said. "We're going to meet Squall and the rest of the Nor'easters at the corner of Walker Street and Cortlandt Alley. We'll have to get to Two and take a bus from there. We need to make sure the path is safe first. Cordy? We're gonna need some ghostly help."

"Charlie? You here?" She looked around the passageway.

A pale, translucent man wearing a business suit appeared in front of her. He looked as solid as a human being, but his skin and clothes were grey and silver, and there was a glow around his silhouette as if he were not entirely there, which was because he wasn't. He appeared to be in his late thirties, but Jack could not be certain. The ghost had a handsome face. His hair was neatly styled, and his eyes were commanding, but pleasant. They all knew who he was—Charles Dupree, who had been killed at a dinner party several decades ago. He was one of the uncommon ghosts whom Cordy had befriended and who came to her wherever she was. Usually she was only capable of summoning a spirit who had died or was buried within a few yards of where she stood.

However, Charles was different. He did not mind being brought back from the afterlife. In fact, he enjoyed helping the Dusk Walkers. Modern objects like televisions and smart phones fascinated him, unlike other ghosts, who preferred to avoid technology.

"I would appreciate it if you didn't call me Charlie, Miss Cordy." He smiled kindly, although Jack recognized sadness creasing his brow.

She returned the smile. "I'm sorry, Charles."

"Much better. What can I help you with?"

"We need to know how safe it is between here and Cortlandt Alley. We'll catch the bus for most of the trip, but are there any patrolmen we might run into while we walk?"

The ghost vanished. This was normal to Cordy, who had grown used to seeing ghosts. The specters had always been around, lurking in the shadows, driving their loved ones insane if they tried to visit them. She was different from everyone else because of the Explosion, able to be the one to call the ghosts instead of them calling her.

Cordy waited patiently for Charles to return, rocking back and forth on the balls of her feet. Jack, Eva, Lily, and Alix tried to remain just as calm. They did not spend as much time speaking to ghosts and were still spooked by their friend's spirit buddies. Jack did not like to mention it, but whenever he saw a ghost, he felt the hairs on his arm raise, and he had the sudden urge to run out of the room. Naturally, he stayed put, since he did not want to offend Cordy or the ghost in question. Also, he did not want to seem like a wimp. Alix, who was ten years old and put her hands over her ears whenever he swore, stood her ground. Compared to her, it would look bad if he decided not to stay.

Charles reappeared in front of Cordy. She was used to this and was the only one who did not jump in surprise. She shot a quick condescending smirk at her companions. Jack rolled his eyes at her before she returned her attention to Charles.

"There are two guards on patrol near the border, but as soon as you are past them, you can walk to Queensboro Plaza and take the subway to Canal Street. From there, you can walk to Cortlandt Alley and arrive on schedule."

"Thanks, Charles." The ghost disappeared again.

"Here's our chance, then. Let's go," said Jack.

The patrolmen were indeed on Queens Boulevard, just next to the border between Districts Two and Three. The Dusk Walkers looked at a wanted poster that was taped to the brick wall of the building nearby. It looked like one of the Dusk Walkers. From the distance where he stood, Jack could not tell whom. When they were just around the corner from the cops, Eva turned to Jack, and he gave her a thumbs-up.

She crept toward the patrolmen without making a single sound in a way that would make a ninja proud. Their backs were to her, and they seemed completely oblivious to the girl behind them until she tapped the larger man's shoulder. He turned around and his eyes widened.

"You!" he exclaimed. That was the only word he was

able to say before Eva punched him in his face. He groaned sharply and backed away. He reached for his walkie-talkie, but before he could press a button, she slammed him headfirst into the wall behind him. The guard crumpled to the ground and blinked once, then his eyes slid shut. He must have had a hundred pounds on her, but she had effortlessly knocked him out cold.

Eva had acted in about five seconds, which was the time that the other cop had taken to draw his handgun. He aimed it at her, and Jack nearly leapt forward in an attempt to shield her from the bullet, but she had it all under control. She swung a roundhouse kick into the cop's ribs, and he doubled over in pain. Then she rammed his skull into the wall as well, and he fell next to his partner.

Cordy, Lily, and Alix high-fived Eva, and Jack squatted next to the policemen. They did not look severely injured, only unconscious. When the short celebration was over, Eva helped Jack drag the cops behind two large trash bins, which brought him relief. The unconscious men did not appear so, but they were quite heavy. Jack did not spend his free time lifting weights. Even if he did, it would not make a difference. His muscles would simply return to how they originally were.

"Good job, Ev," Jack said when they were done. She winked at him and joined the others. For a stupid little moment, he felt giddy inside. A smile tugged at the corner of his lips, and then he shook it off. They had business to do, and he had to focus.

He waved for his companions to follow him down the boulevard. They had not walked two blocks when they passed a wanted poster on the pole of a grimy streetlamp. The poster bore three different pictures of his face, all taken from security cameras over the past three years. Jack smiled. Part of him enjoyed that the three Hunters and all of the patrolmen in the streets were looking for them instead of real criminals such as rapists or murderers. Perhaps the rumors on the radio were correct: The government had completely gone to the dogs after the Explosion.

"Those pictures suck." He crossed his arms and scowled. In the pictures, there were no good angles of his face. They were stretched in ways that made his face wider or thinner, and neither looked good.

Eva scoffed and tore down the poster, revealing the advertisement for a local rock band underneath it. She tossed it to Jack, who caught it. "Can we go now?"

CHAPTER THREE

The Dusk Walkers split up on the subway. Eva, Lily, and Alix went to the first car while Jack and Cordy sat on separate benches in the next. Beside him sat a girl their age, a tower of books in her lap. Her bleached hair contrasted deeply with her dark skin, and sparkly blue eye-shadow and hot-pink blush masked her face. Fishnet tights were cut off at the ankles just above oversized black boots. Jack smiled at Cordy. This girl was just her type. Cordy whistled sharply. The girl with the big boots glanced up. Cordy dragged her tongue slowly across her top lip and blew a kiss. The girl arched an eyebrow, her purple lips stretching into a smirk.

Jack decided to leave them alone. He winked at Cordy and stood as the subway slowed to a stop, swinging his bag onto his shoulder as he waited for the doors to open. When he stepped out, he merely turned to his left and jumped into the first car of the same subway. Inside, he spotted Lily and Alix chatting in the corner while Eva leaned against the metal pole in the center. All the seats were filled, so Jack quickly rushed to stand next to her.

"Hey," she said. He blinked, his jaw hanging slightly slack. Looking at her, he saw an enormous contrast between her and Cordy's new friend. Eva wore no makeup, instead letting the green sweater she wore bring out the color of her eyes. The cotton garment was loose on her shoulders, and he could see parts of the black tank top she wore underneath. Her tight-fitting khaki shorts reached her knees, and thick woolen socks peeked out from her brown boots. "Jack?"

"Huh?" He raised his eyes from, his face flushing as he realized, her legs.

"Where's Cordy?"

Jack cleared his throat. "Uh…she's in the other car. With a new friend."

Eva shot him a disapproving look. "What are the house rules?"

"Don't hang out with strangers, along with an entire novel's worth of other stuff," said Jack, knowing that he exaggerated. "We're getting off at the next stop anyway. You can scold her when we step off."

"I still don't approve of her thing with Thunderhead," said Eva. He knew that she referred to Cordy's not-so-secret lover from the Nor'easters, and he nodded. "They aren't right for each other."

Jack said nothing, hoping that Eva thought that he was right for her. When the subway slowed, he motioned for Lily and Alix to stand. He pocketed his hands and waited for the doors to open. After they finished meeting with the Nor'easters, he and the Dusk Walkers would hopefully be able to break into a store and fill up on food for the next week. From what he knew, Lily only had a bag of gummy worms and a sandwich that they had stolen from kiosks a few days ago, and she was always the one who had the most food. Jack only had a bag of potato chips crushed underneath his spare boxers.

"Jay, this is Gwen," said Cordy to Jack when he arrived at her side. The girl with the big black boots, who now stood very close to Cordy, threw him a quick jut of the chin in salute.

"Who's this?" said Gwen. Her voice was rough and deep, but Jack did not feel any bad vibes from her. She was unlikely to be a police officer in disguise, which was his only real concern. "Boyfriend? Brother?"

"Both," said Cordy with a grin, bumping her narrow hipbone into his. "He's my best friend."

"Sweet. Well, call me when you can, mystery girl," said Gwen, handing Cordy a slip of paper before walking through the station. Jack nodded to himself. Gwen seemed nice, although he doubted Cordy would call her back. She never could.

"Are you both idiots?" hissed Eva. Jack whirled around, caught off guard. She, Lily, and Alix emerged from their hiding place among the thinning crowds of the station. "What if she knows who we are?"

"D'you think she recognized us?" said Lily.

"She's from Little Rock," said Cordy. "She's only in the area to visit her cousin. If she knows about us, I doubt she recognized our faces."

Before Eva could retort, Jack nervously interrupted her. "If she had recognized us, I doubt she would've been so Zen about it. I mean, most people either try to beat us up or they run away screaming, don't they?"

"Yeah." Lily shrugged. "Forget about it. Let's go, we'll be late. And you know how Squall can get when he's angry."

"Right." Jack cringed. Squall was prone to hitting things with his bare fists when his temper was high. It was a sight to behold, especially when his victim was a brick wall. "Let's go." They hurried out of the station and onto the streets. The walk to their meeting place would take no longer than five minutes.

Cortlandt Alley was nearly empty at that time of the evening, since it was the territory of the Nor'easters. The Dusk Walkers had free passage, but Jack still remained cautious, keeping a careful tab on his surroundings. A car drove by. The sour gas that the engine left behind faded gradually. The lights in the buildings around had all gone dim. The city that never used to sleep had finally taken a rest.

"Bout damn time ye got 'ere." The height-lacking, fedora-wearing man known as Squall emerged from the adjoining building, closely followed by four others. Tempest, his red-haired right-hand woman, stood behind Squall. Thunderhead's boots announced her presence before her face did, but her squat nose and high forehead were soon illuminated by the streetlamps. Zephyr came next, his shaved head glinting in the light. Another man followed, his blond hair a messy mop on top of his head. Jack did not recognize him. He cleared his throat and addressed Squall.

"Sorry for the hold-up. Won't happen again."

"Where were ya?"

"Well, you know how bad traffic can be around here." Apparently it had once been impossible to drive anywhere in the city without being held up on the streets. Jack did not remember. He only knew the now.

"Whatever," said Squall. He gave a scoff and looked away. For now, his fists were at his side. "Cy, introduce yourself."

The new blond man strolled up to Jack. He was several inches taller than the Dusk Walker, and Jack struggled to keep his expression still as he looked upward. "I'm Cyclone. And I've gotta say, you're a lot tinier than I expected."

Jack hoped the heat he felt in his neck was not visible. "Well, you know what they say." He narrowed his eyes, balling his fists in frustration. "Power comes in small packages."

"Really, now?" Cyclone was closer now, and Jack could smell the cocaine on his foul breath. "What other small packages d'you got, Turner?" Cyclone looked downward pointedly.

Jack raised an eyebrow and laughed, releasing some of his anger. He broke his gaze from Cyclone, the mocking glare in the other's eyes infuriating him further. Tempest and Zephyr stepped forward to pull back their companion, but Cyclone shrugged them off. Jack felt his friends fidget behind him, but he stood his ground as Cyclone gave him a tiny shove. Jack knew that it was a test. He would not give Cyclone the pleasure of seeing him crack just yet, despite how tempted he was.

"Don't touch him," said Alix.

"It's okay, Al."

"Cy, that's enough," warned Tempest. Jack knew they were both thinking the same thing. If a fight erupted between the Dusk Walkers and the Nor'easters, their alliance would be over.

"This is my only problem with joining: dealing with the most feared criminals in the city. But what's to fear?" Cyclone narrowed his eyes at Jack. "The Dusk Walkers. A stupid name that you didn't even make up. You're just a kid who can't get hurt, and his bitches."

It was as though a bomb went off.

Jack could not restrain his frustration, and he shoved Cyclone backward with enough force to send him stumbling into Zephyr. There was a series of growls—Lily was now a lion, leaping at Cyclone with bared teeth. Cordy advanced to help her, keeping Zephyr and Tempest at bay with her bony fists. Jack reached for his knife, but a hand closed around his wrist.

"You don't want to make things worse," said Eva, her eyes boring into his. The look alone froze him in his tracks. "Wait here."

Jack knew it would not look better for him if he remained behind as the others fought, but he also knew Eva would have everything under control in a few moments. He put himself to use and turned to Alix. She stood with her arms folded over her chest, her shoulders slack.

"You all right?"

Alix nodded and looked around him. Lily sat on top of Cyclone's chest in her feline form. Cordy stood over his head, her hands on her hips.

"Who's the bitch now?" Her smirk fell as Eva pulled them off their offender.

"Why don't we all just take a breather?" said Eva, turning from Cyclone to the rest of the Nor'easters. "Let's go our separate ways. For now, at least. We can discuss our agreement later. Next week, same time?"

"Fine," said Cyclone. He clambered to his feet, glaring at Jack as he did so. "This pussy would rather hide behind his girls than stick up for himself."

"Don't," said Jack, reaching out to grip Cordy's shoulder as she flipped off the older men.

She whirled around to face him, her thick hair whipping his cheek. "You aren't going to take his crap, are you?"

"I'm not." He wanted to add that attacking the Nor'easters would show that Cyclone's words were affecting them, but he knew Cordy would tell him off for brown-nosing Eva. He ended his sentence after two words.

Sirens filled the air and the red-and-blue lights of a police car flashed against the graffitied walls. Jack had learned not to think when they were cornered, but to run. It was possible that the car was not for them, but for the gang that they were leaving behind. Either way, the Dusk Walkers were capable of hiding from normal cops. They were not normal criminals. He gripped Cordy's wrist and pulled her down the street. They still needed to pick up more supplies for the next week. He knew of a nearby grocery store and headed in its direction.

Once the five of them ran at a decent pace, Eva took the lead with her longer legs and endurance. The sirens did not grow closer, and Jack could no longer see the Nor'easters. Perhaps they had been too slow and had been arrested. Jack hoped Cyclone had been taken into custody, and then they could return to their previously arranged treaty.

"Let's split up. Just in case the cops are still around," said Eva when they arrived on an empty street. Jack nodded, an irritable cramp forming in his side. If the five of them remained in a group, they were slower and easier to identify. Lily morphed into a kitten and crawled into Alix's arms.

"Are you going with them?" Jack looked at Eva, his insides twisting. It was such a little thing, but lately she chose to remain with the two younger Dusk Walkers when they split into groups. He could not help but wonder if there was something about him that Eva disliked.

"Yeah," she said, ushering Alix toward the street corner. "We'll meet you at the store."

Jack frowned, but knew they could not linger. Eva, Lily, and Alix hurried to the left while he and Cordy continued forward. They swung under metal construction bars and past late-night workers. Cordy dashed across the seat of a wooden bench near a bundle of trees. They ducked their heads as they rushed past a police station. Jack knew Districts Two and Three well enough to identify the main streets and to find the nearest coffee shop. District One was less familiar to him, but the Dusk Walkers tried to avoid it as much as possible, since there was not much there that interested them, and tighter authority meant putting their safety at risk.

Once they were on a busy street, they slowed down in order to act as normal civilians would. Jack adjusted the bag on his back and stuffed his hands into the pockets of his sweater. Cordy looped her arm through his, bumping her forehead against his shoulder before grinning up at him. "You okay? The new guy back there wasn't so nice."

He scoffed. "Of course I'm fine. I'm always fine."

She rolled her eyes. "That's very cute, but I know all your secrets."

"Ooh, scary," he said as she smacked her lips on his jaw, her heels landing on the sidewalk again. Jack chuckled and wrapped his arm around her waist, pulling their hips together. "But I don't have any secrets. I can't keep anything from you, Ghost-Whisperer, no matter how much I try."

They continued through the streets and through the thinning throng of New Yorkers. The two of them were nearly silent for the rest of the walk, only pointing out things like odd graffiti or hot-pink cars. They arrived in front of the store, and Eva, Lily, and Alix were waiting for them against the bicycle racks. "What took you so long?"

"Jack decided to go the long way," said Cordy, removing her arm from around his.

"Hey, you didn't say anything about it!" He frowned at her and she kicked him, causing his eyes to water. Jack looked around. The Dusk Walkers were the only people in the street. The store was already closed. Eva often refused to break into a store that was still occupied because she did not enjoy risking other peoples' safety. It was only when they were desperately in need of something and they had no other option that they would commit an open robbery.

Jack tried not to stare at the building, having caught a glimpse of a security camera. He walked in the direction of the park nearby and leaned close to Lily. "I've got a mission for you. Sneak through that side door and find the room where the cameras are operated. Shut down everything, find the security code, then disable the alarm system. Can you do that?"

She stared at him for a moment, memorizing the instructions. "Yeah, I think. How do I disable the alarm?"

"You punch in the code."

"Right. Be back in a sec." Lily glanced at the camera

once, then hurried toward the park, disappearing into the dark. If she were to abruptly transform into some sort of creature while the cameras watched, suspicion would certainly be aroused before Jack and the others could even get close to the building. They could not risk setting off the alarm, for a police station was not far away. Once the police would be alerted of a break-in caused by the Dusk Walkers, the Hunters would be called immediately, and Luke Warren would arrive on the scene in only moments.

"It's the usual run, isn't it? Or do we need anything else?" Eva was so close to him now, as she came to his side, that Jack could almost feel the energy between them. He could not yet determine whether it was the force of his resolute attraction or her possible repulsion, but it was certainly there. Her hair fell straight that night, secured in her usual ponytail. A strand hung loose by her ear, and he fought the urge to push it back for her. Her pale head was held high and haughty, and her eyes were half-closed in the flare of the streetlamp. Her arms were folded tightly over her chest. He noticed for the first time that her green sweater did not look quite so warm, but he did not see her shiver.

"Umm…yeah," he said. His voice sounded especially high-pitched. "Yeah, just the usual run." They would make their way into the store and retrieve items from the four food groups: sweets, energy bars, liquids, and miscellaneous substantial things. Jack more often than not occupied himself by dallying around the front of the store while he searched for any other necessities. For example, he was in need of a new toothbrush, and Lily trusted him in choosing a new novel for her to read. He considered a mystery this time, because the previous month she had insisted on a romance that she had not enjoyed.

Jack leaned against the black metal fence that surrounded the park, making sure to face away from the security cameras. The others did the same, forming a row along the barrier. He hoped Lily would not take much longer to finish her task, or something would be wrong.

"Eeek!"

CHAPTER FOUR

Alix's shriek bounced off the sleeping city like a rubber ball. Jack's hand went reflexively to his knife as he turned to see what had happened. A great big lemur, as lean as a branch, had crawled onto the young girl's back. Its brown eyes bulged from its skull and Jack scoffed, knowing now that the creature was no threat. The lemur grew slowly into Lily as she stepped back, relieving Alix of her weight.

"Not funny, Lily!" whined Alix.

"Was, too." The older girl gave a low chortle. She then looked sheepishly to Eva, who shook her head in disapproval. "Coast's clear. We can go in now."

"Did you take out the cameras?" said Jack.

"Duh. I'm not as incompetent as you think I am."

He huffed, putting his arm around Lily's shoulders. "You're not incont...incop...in..."

"—Competent," said Eva. She strolled haughtily past them and toward the store, Cordy and Alix following suit. Jack blew out his flushed cheeks and cast a quick glance at Lily, who shrugged.

"You'd better step up your game if you wanna get into her pants."

"What?" He stumbled and followed Lily toward the side door of the building. She had left a wooden wedge there to keep the door open for them.

Alix turned on the lights inside the store, illuminating tiled floors that reflected their faces and a vast space for the five of them to roam about. As would a wolf, Jack grinned hungrily at the sight of aisles and aisles of food. His mouth watered and he swallowed to stop himself from drooling.

They split up. Cordy accompanied Alix to fetch enough bottled liquids to last them a week, and Eva and Lily searched for non-perishable meals. Jack knew that Cordy and Lily would also take care of refilling the group's stash of sweets and pastries, so he did not bother with those. He would instead go to the front of the store to find a toothbrush and Lily's book.

While he considered what else they could need, he headed through the drink aisle. Alix lowered several bottles of water into her backpack until she could fit no more. When Cordy took a liter of soda from the shelf, the younger girl frowned.

"That's not good for you," Alix said in a singsong voice, wiggling a finger at her.

Cordy scoffed and put the cream soda back, taking apple juice instead. "Is this better?"

"Much."

Jack laughed while he walked past them, making his way toward the pharmaceutical aisle. He chose a standard green toothbrush and put it into his bag. The mystery novel was the next on his list of things to retrieve, and he went to the cashier stands for that. The racks hosted a small number of paperback books. As he flipped through the pages of one of them, he caught a flash of something in the trash bin behind the cashier. Returning the book to its place, he climbed over the booth and picked up the magazine.

He sat atop the counter, scrolling through the glossy sheets. He felt incredibly naughty for even touching the thing, but he was a teenage boy, after all. Keeping his eyes locked on the pages, he reached to his right for one of the chocolate bars that waited for him on the racks.

"Ouch!" He tore his gaze away from the magazine and saw Eva standing next to him. "Did you slap my arm?"

She held out her hand, palm to the sky. "Gimme the porn, perv."

"Nah…" He leapt into the booth and held it in the air tauntingly. Despite the two of them being the same height, his arms were longer than hers, and the counter that stood between them protected him. "It's way too hardcore for you, Blondie."

Eva scoffed and raised a pale eyebrow. "Fine," she said. "If you want to be that way…" With the speed of a predator hunting its prey, she swung herself over the counter and into the booth. With the two of them trapped in the tiny space, she was able to twist his arm painfully, forcing him to release the magazine. She picked it up before he could reach it, a smirk playing on her lips. She stuffed it back into the trash bin, stomping on it a few times to crush it to the bottom. Jack gave an humiliated huff and contented himself with being thankful that none of the others had seen them.

Police sirens cut through the air and red-and-blue lights flashed through the barred windows at the front of the store. Those lights struck dread in Jack's mind and a shiver crawled down his spine.

"They must have seen us on the cameras before Lily shut them down," said Eva. "I keep telling you guys that we should wear disguises or something, but you never listen. And I would look like an idiot if I did it on my own."

While she had the time for logic and reasoning, Jack's instincts and adrenaline kicked in. As soon as Cordy, Lily, and Alix emerged from between the aisles, he waved to get their attention. The five of them raced through the store, knocking over towers of crackers along the way, and they burst into the stockroom. A voice spoke through a megaphone outside, but Jack did not listen to the words. He could only make sure his four companions were with him as they raced out the door.

"N-Y-P-D, don't move!" Jack ignored the words of a second voice, only using it to know the location of the cops. They were on foot. The Dusk Walkers could outrun them. They raced around the back of the grocery store.

"Go, go, go!" Eva was shouting. Jack turned to see what the ruckus was about. Before his eyes could even focus on the three fleeing figures, a firm grip dragged him away. He struggled to release his wrist, then recognized Eva's fingers around his arm. She let him go. "Run faster," she said. "To the street."

"More cops will be there!"

"That's the point." Even though they were running, he saw that she was worried. Her eyebrows were drawn together and her lips were twisted in a frown. "We're the decoys. I'm sorry. I wasn't thinking quickly enough before. You should have gone with the others through the park."

"No," he choked as they emerged from the rear of the building. He envied her ability to speak clearly while running. "No, I'm glad to…to be here."

"Look! Two of them, there!" Car doors slammed shut and sirens resumed. More cops were coming.

"Away from the road," said Jack. They could run and hide from the officers who were on foot, but they hardly stood a chance against a vehicle.

Eva said nothing, instead tugging on the straps of his backpack, leading him into a parking garage. He wanted to ask how this would help their situation, but he was incapable of forming a coherent sentence. "Up!"

"Up?" He glanced around. He found one concrete slope that led downward. Soon after, he spotted another that went the other way. He and Eva raced upward with long strides and quick breaths. She did not seem to have a problem, but he began to tire after the second floor.

"Come on! I'm not leaving you to them."

His head buzzed at her encouragement, helping him to continue running despite the burning in his thighs and the tightness in his chest. By the time they had made it to the roof, a cramp in his side caused him to double over. He gripped his knees to support himself, wiping the cold sweat from his forehead with his sleeve. Eva raced around the area, weaving in between the cars, searching for something he did not know. "Why are we up here? Isn't it the last place we should be?"

"Yes…and no," she muttered. "I hope the others got out all right."

He nodded, his heart rate rapidly returning to its normal pace. He stood to help her. "What are you looking for?"

Her shoes crunched on the broken asphalt under their feet as she peered over the ledge. "We're surrounded."

"Great."

"How many cops followed us?"

"No more than two or three," he said, remembering the popeyed man and the woman with the straight dark hair. He could not quite remember if there was another. "They'll be here any second."

Eva shrugged, still looking at the streets below. "I can take two or three."

"But what are we doing here?" He jutted out his chin

impatiently, limping to her location. They were only four stories above the ground, but he still disliked their situation. "Maybe I can help—whoa! What are you doing?"

She climbed onto the ledge, standing dozens of feet above the ground below. "Stay put and play along."

His eyes widened. Although she seemed perfectly balanced, he was still afraid for her. He saw no way that this could be a good thing. "You might want to get down from there."

She lifted her right foot and he sucked in a gasp. She brought it around her other foot, turning to face him. Her back was to the outside. Perspiration gathered in his balled fists and his heartbeat was raised once again. He appeared to be the only one who was concerned.

Eva's composure was unmoving. She swung her backpack off her shoulders and onto the asphalt in front of him. Her arms rose from her sides, forming a cross position. She shot him a confident smile that made him dig his fingernails into his palms, nearly drawing blood.

"Knife," she said. Jack almost asked what she meant by the word, then tentatively drew his blade from his belt. She nodded and he gripped it tight.

"Turner! Edwards! Drop the knife, get down from the ledge, and put your hands up in the air!" Two police officers arrived on the roof, guns at the ready.

Jack froze, wondering when exactly Eva's plan would come into use. He glanced at her, and she did not raise her hands from where they were, perpendicular to the rest of her body. He followed her lead, remaining calm and keeping a firm grasp on his knife.

"Hands. Up." The woman looked nearly as threatening as Eva could when she tried. Jack was almost tempted to obey. The cop stepped forward, and his muscles tightened. He and Eva were trapped, and they all knew it.

"Why?" said Eva, still composed. "You won't shoot. Even if it's not fatal, I'll fall off this building. I doubt the Hunters would appreciate that."

Jack made an effort to keep his jaw from dropping open. He turned to stare at her with widened eyes. They both knew that the cops were aware of his own abilities. On more than one occasion, the girls had been spared, and he had been the target of the gunfire. "Ev, I don't think—"

The female officer appeared to have thought the same way. Her firearm slowly turned to a different angle, now pointing at Jack's chest. His hands raised themselves, but he still had the knife. Eva tensed at his side. "If you shoot him, I'll kill you both."

"We won't hurt either of you if you just step down from the ledge."

Eva lowered her arms to her sides, stuffing them into her pockets. Jack was almost relieved that she was coming down, until she threw her left foot backward. It hovered over the street below. "You didn't specify which way."

The popeyed cop advanced to the other's side. "Captain, shouldn't we wait?"

As soon as the female turned her head, Eva attacked. Jack was not quite sure what had happened, because it went by so quickly. She took two strides, and she was off the ledge and onto the police captain. Jack was left with the man. A quick glance told him that the other's finger was moving toward the trigger of the gun. Jack ducked, and the man fired, the shot missing by a mile.

Knife throwing was not a specialty of his, but he could always do with some practice. After some experimentation on her own, Eva had taught him a few tricks with his knife. While the cop was taking aim, he shuffled forward and swung the blade at the man's gun hand. The weapons scattered across the roof, and Jack charged, ramming his shoulder into the other's gut as he leaned to retrieve the knife and the handgun. He pointed the firearm at the cop while he set the blade against his own skin, keeping it at a safe angle.

"We'll make a deal with you," said Jack. It was his turn to take control of the situation. He tried not to let his hand tremble under the uncomfortable weight of the weapon. Despite its warmth, he felt a sudden frostiness when he touched the thing.

"We don't make deals," said the woman, trapped under Eva's foot.

He gave her a condescending glance, nothing more. "If you let us go, we'll let you go. And if you don't, well, I'll leave that up to your imagination, because you will let us go."

"How can you be so sure?"

Jack smiled darkly, but it was just an act. "Oh, I'm sure all right. You wouldn't risk the life of your officer, would you…" He glanced at the nameplate on her uniform. "Captain Pizzi?"

CHAPTER FIVE

At nine o'clock in the evening, the Dusk Walkers had not yet broken into the grocery store in District Two. They were still with the Nor'easters, but the Hunters did not know that.

The door to Luke Warren's apartment clicked shut as he returned from work. It was his birthday. His team had been let off early for the occasion, but was not as though they were kept on their toes every night in the first place.

A smile tugged at his lips as he turned on the lights with the help of his self-generated electricity. Gianna had told him to stop doing that, but she was a technopath. She could fix whatever he had broken. At least he was the one to thank for the very small amount of energy bills to pay. He also possessed superhuman speed, allowing him to run to work instead of borrowing Gianna's car. He was an awful driver and could not be bothered to change that.

He went to the mirror to make sure his hair was as rebellious as it should be. Despite his co-workers often informing him that the style went against regulations and threatening to cut it off while he slept, he had lasted long enough with his locks still intact. The strands were of considerable length, and they stuck up in all directions, forming a messy but coordinated nest on top of his head. There was no gel involved. Instead, his hair received any excess static electricity that he had accumulated and levitated on its own.

Luke heard the door to the apartment open and he turned around. Gianna closed the door behind her. "You're early."

"You're complaining," she said, dropping her purse on the kitchen counter and hopping up to give him a quick kiss on his cheek. The rims of her thick black glasses pressed against his temple and he got a whiff of her perfume. Its name escaped him, but he thought it smelled rather like saltwater and coconut. "Happy twenty-seventh, handsome."

"How's M-G?" said Luke when she turned to clear the magazines and beer cans from the coffee table. For the occasion, Gianna, who was four years his junior, had invited their closest friends to pay them a visit. Marial Grace, also known by her initials, was a colleague of theirs who lived on the floor below. She was a scientist who was in the middle of some major research concerning the Explosion.

"She's great. But she pulled the graveyard shift at the lab, so she isn't coming." Gianna tossed the magazines in the recycling bin and stowed the cans in an empty cabinet. She stood and froze, her wide lips parted carefully and her eyes narrowed. "Were you messing with the lights again?"

"No..." Luke pulled a face and scratched behind his ear. His hair reacted in accordance to his mood. A crackle came from one of the spikes at the base of his neck.

"Uh huh." She smirked and leaned over the counter, propping her elbows against the granite. She snapped her fingers and the lights were suddenly brighter. "You didn't do 'em right."

His only punishment was another kiss. No sooner had her lips brushed his, she pulled back.

"There goes the doorbell," she said, the dimple in her left cheek as prominent as ever. "You wanna get that?"

Luke went to the front door before the buzzer even rang. As soon as the doorknob turned, a friendly, albeit enthusiastic voice met him. "It's the giraffe! Haven't seen you in weeks!"

"I'm pretty sure we spoke on Wednesday." Teddy Gladstone was a homicide detective with the NYPD, and his wife Eliza was a nurse at the hospital near the precinct. Normally Luke disliked other cops, but every so often he and Teddy would have a coffee together, and a friendship had formed.

Teddy pulled him down for a hug before entering the apartment, and Luke leaned down to kiss Eliza on her cheek. Just as he was about to close the door, Rae materialized on the welcoming mat, not startling him as much as it would a normal person. He rolled his eyes.

"Hey you," she said, her head cocked lightly to the side. She had already changed out of her work clothes and wore a purple pleather jacket over a rock band T-shirt. "Were you on paper duty today?"

"It was worse than being buried alive. How was your training?"

She gave a shrug. "Not bad. I kicked that heavy bag's ass good and proper."

Rae was only twenty years old, which meant that she was technically too young to be a police officer. Nevertheless, she still participated on their hunts, getting personal tutoring and training during the day, when the Dusk Walkers were inactive. When Luke and Gianna were not doing the same as their peer, they studied published theories about the aftereffects of the Explosion and documents about the Dusk Walkers. So far, there was nothing certain, apart from what they had gathered about the children's past lives and what the Hunters knew. They would have to wait until they had at least one of the teenagers in custody.

"Rae, darling, feel free to shove past my boyfriend for leaving you out in the cold for this long," said Gianna, handing two beers to Teddy and Eliza.

Rae shuffled into the apartment, away from the cold of the hallway. Luke closed the door, and she was already in the kitchen, rummaging around the back of the refrigerator for her reserved case of cola. She did not drink alcohol out of preference, not age, so she kept her own stash of beverages in their home for such an occasion.

"Is this everybody?" said Rae, emerging from behind the appliance's door with a can in her hand. She reached next for a mug in which to pour the drink.

"Yeah. M-G couldn't make it."

"This is some lame birthday party, dude," said Teddy. He, Eliza, and Rae crowded onto the couch, and Gianna sat in one of the chairs facing the coffee table. Luke took a seat in the second chair. He took the beer that she held out for him.

"All right, you can throw it next time."

"I will! Just you wait. Next year will be mind-blowing!"

"It's on."

Teddy nodded, accepting the challenge. Judging by the pensive look on his face, he was already planning what he would do 364 days from then.

"A toast," said Eliza while her husband continued to ponder. "Happy birthday, Luke. We wish you many more."

They all leaned forward to tap their beverages together and drank. Teddy was the first to speak. "So spill. How do you three feel about being called the superheroes of New York in that magazine last weekend?"

Gianna scoffed. "I feel objectified." Luke nodded in agreement.

"Naw, I'm serious! Think about what makes a superhero: You've got the powers, you've got the angst, and you save the people!"

"We don't save people," said Luke before taking

another drink.

"You protect the city from those Dusk Douches, right?"

"Well, yeah—"

Teddy put up his hands for Luke to stop talking. "I rest my case."

"All right, whatever. At least we don't wear spandex."

When the phone rang, Luke frowned. This could not be good. It was either someone wishing him a happy birthday or the Hunters had a job to do. Both ideas discouraged him greatly. He and Rae looked to Gianna, who as a technopath, could tell who was calling.

"It's Roy."

Impatient groans followed her announcement. Stanley Roy was the police captain in charge of the trio. Although he did not possess any special abilities, he was experienced in organized crime, which was not dissimilar from their search for the Dusk Walkers. Luke appreciated Roy, but the only reason their superior would call was if he had a lead on the pesky little ankle-biters. If so, the party was cancelled.

Luke picked up the ringing phone from the coffee table. "Hello?"

"It's Captain Roy. Are you busy right now?"

"No, Sir. At least, it's nothing important." He cast an

apologetic glance to Gianna, who was able to hear what both men were saying, as opposed to the others, who could only hear Luke. "What's going on?"

"Two of the Dusk Walkers have been cornered on the roof of the parking garage on Harrison Street: Turner and Edwards."

Luke almost grinned. Sometimes he could not help but think of the Dusk Walkers as collector's items. It was how many people spoke of them, and he had accidentally picked up the habit. Jack Turner and Eva Edwards were the most valuable pieces of the set because of their abilities. Scientists desperately wanted to get their hands on both of them in particular. If they could find out what exactly made the two teenagers heal so quickly and endure so much, a number of cures and drugs could be envisioned afterward. "Do you know what happened?" he said into the phone. "It's not like them to be caught by street patrols."

"You've got the local grocery store to thank for that. The new surveillance system they set up came in handy. The Dusk Walkers were recognized before they could even turn off the cameras," said Roy.

"We'll be on Harrison ASAP. I'll let you know how it plays out."

"Be careful, Warren. And don't hurt the kids—give them a chance to come quietly. It would look better for you and me."

"Of course, Sir." He hung up. He would try his best to obey the order, but due to the tenacity of the Dusk

Walkers, it was much easier said than done. "We've got to go," he announced to Rae and the Gladstones.

Glass mugs were set on the table and the five of them stood. "It's too bad," said Eliza. "We never get to hang out together. Maybe some other time?"

"Absolutely." While Luke and his partners collected their necessities from the front hall closet—handcuffs, guns, and night-vision goggles—Teddy and Eliza let themselves out. He would have to get back at them later for stealing his beer.

Luke, Gianna, and Rae made sure that they had their badges with them. They were usually recognized by their faces alone, but they could not afford to generalize those who would be waiting at the crime scene. Luke pulled on his shoes and was ready long before the other two.

"We'll catch up. Go ahead," said Gianna. He knew she and Rae would take the car from the garage to get to Harrison Street. He kissed her cheek and was out the door in a flash, almost literally. If he arrived in time to hold off Jack and Eva, perhaps Gianna and Rae could find the other Dusk Walkers. Knowing how close the children were, the three missing youngsters would not be far behind.

The path to his destination was clear for the most part, thank heavens. He did not want to experience crashing into a person when he raced at dozens of miles per hour. Down avenues, across streets, his superhuman speed carried him to the front of the parking garage, which police cars efficiently surrounded. Yellow tape fenced off the scene while the spectators stared up at the building.

He slowed to a stop near the closest officer. "Who's your captain?"

"Rosa Pizzi," said the man with the bulbous nose. "Why?"

"Why isn't she here?"

"She's up on the roof."

"Thanks." Luke made his way through Pizzi's crew and into the garage. He hurried up the concrete slopes, the twenty-four-hour lit lamps illuminating his path.

☢

Jack and Eva moved Captain Pizzi and the officer against the ledge. They held the cops at gunpoint, making sure their captives' hands were raised well into the air and that their radios were disconnected. It was not long before Jack grew bored, and he sat on the ground, holding the pistol with two hands.

"Why hasn't anyone else come for us yet? It's not like we're going anywhere." As soon as he spoke, a coldness shaped inside of his stomach. They would be caught. He had always thought of himself as invincible, but he had slipped up. Somewhere along the way to the store, they had spoiled their routine, and an alarm had gone off. He was far from invincible.

"Luke will be here any second," said Eva. "That's who they're waiting for."

Jack nodded nervously and handed her his acquired

gun, reaching for his own knife. He was not frightened of firearms. He just hated them. They were unfair, and they were even cowardly. Guns harmed from a distance, as opposed to knives, which were up close and personal. They took more guts to use, but Jack did not concern himself with that factor. He used his blade for purely defensive purposes, of course. No life had ever been taken with it by his hand.

He stood, glad to be rid of the gun. Eva did not look at him, her focus concentrated on the two police officers. Jack swung his backpack off one shoulder and strode toward the ledge of the roof, where he dropped it. He cleared his throat and resumed speaking. "You'd expect there to be more sirens and helicopters, wouldn't you? Or aren't we important enough for that?"

"They probably don't want us to think we are," said Eva. She glanced over her shoulder to him and he managed a smile. She returned the favor, then stiffened. "Wait."

"What?"

"Did you hear something?"

He listened. The sounds of car engines below echoed against the surrounding buildings. Jack stared at the sky, hoping to hear what she did. When he did not, he spoke. "What is it?"

Eva frowned, shaking her head. "I don't—"

A weight crushed his throat and he choked, reflexively reaching to free himself. Instead of succeeding, he found his knife hand turned against him, its point pressed between his ribs. When the world stopped spinning, Jack noticed the sickly familiar smell of pine needles and leather. He groaned, closing his eyes. "Goddamn super speed." When he blinked his eyes open, he was welcomed by Eva pointing both guns at him. No, not at him, but at Luke Warren, the Hunter.

"Bad idea," said Luke, who had Jack in a chokehold with his right arm and controlled the knife with the other hand.

Jack saw Eva's expression falter. If anyone understood how easy it was to hurt him and to get away with it, it was Luke. She did not drop the guns, but she took her fingers off the triggers.

"Now drop them," said Luke. Jack could not resist flinching as the knife pinched his skin. "Come quietly and we don't have to do this."

Jack and Eva huffed in unison, him a little more nervously. Giving in was never an option for the Dusk Walkers. "Careful, you're outnumbered."

"Not for long," murmured Luke, only loud enough for Jack to hear. His heart raced in desperation for Gianna and Rae to show themselves, if only to know where they were. He had thought too soon.

Eva screamed. The guns in her hands snapped apart, clattering to the ground. Gianna, the technopath, emerged on the roof. She whistled for the two police officers to leave, motioning toward the exit. Eva massaged her fingers, straightened and ran at Gianna.

Jack hoped to use Luke's distraction to escape, but his struggle was in vain. The arm around his neck tightened to the point where it was painful. He gave a start, sucking in a shocked breath as Eva doubled over.

Rae was suddenly visible, shaking out her fists before lifting Eva to her feet by her hair. A bird's screech cut the air, and an unnaturally sized dark shape swooped down upon them. When Luke ducked, Jack slipped out from underneath him and was free. The enormous bird doubled around and went after Luke once more. Jack kicked at Luke's hand and the knife fell into his range. He lunged at it, his fingers only inches away from the handle, then Luke pulled him back by his foot. Luke would not release his ankle despite how close the black-feathered bird came.

Gunshots from Gianna's direction alerted Jack. He whirled around, glancing past Rae and Eva's fight, although he could only see the latter throwing punches at the air. Above him the gigantic bird soared off the roof, away from the gun, and she still flew steadily. That told Jack that she was not hurt. "Lily..." he whispered, only to reassure himself that she was all right.

Luke was fast. Fast enough that Jack hardly had any time to register that Luke had him by the jacket before it was too late. Jack was on his back, his legs folded uselessly underneath him. Something crackled near his ear, and he whirled to stare at it in shock. Luke's hands raced with sparks of electricity, and Jack was pinned. Behind his adversary, he met Eva's eyes.

She held an invisible Rae in a headlock, from what he could tell by her awkward bent-over position. When he looked to her, time slowed. She stared at him with wide eyes. Her hair had fallen into her face, but two flashes of green were distinguishable behind the blond strands. He mustered up the courage to unclench his jaw, and he mouthed a single word: "Go."

Luke's right hand wrapped around Jack's forehead, thumb and index finger on either of his temples. And then pain—only pain piercing him to the bone, and another sound, this time like a struck bell echoing on and on, then nothing else.

CHAPTER SIX

Luke sat up, dread sinking in his chest like a ship's anchor. He had killed Turner. The public would find out sooner or later, and Luke would be a child murderer. No, he was safe. Jack was breathing.

"Is he all right?" said Gianna, kneeling next to him.

Luke felt Jack's spirited, unsteady pulse. He nearly deflated in relief. "He'll be fine." As long as Jack was alive, he could heal later on. "I never tried that before with the electricity." Often, too much electricity accumulated inside of him, giving him migraines and mood swings. Now, nothing. Despite the stressful situation, he felt calmer than he had in weeks.

"Rae's taking care of Eva." Gianna looked at the gun in her hands, forehead creased in concern. "Do you think I hit the bird?"

"I hope you didn't. We'll see if she comes back." He climbed to his feet and she whipped out her radio. "What're you doing?"

"Getting an ambulance." She brought the device to her mouth.

"What, for him? He's going to wake up and be perfectly fine in a few minutes, you know that."

"Then call it insurance in case we do need an ambulance."

The bird screeched once more, tearing his attention away from Rae and Eva. When Luke turned around, Lily was no longer a winged creature, but morphed through the air into a…puma? It did not matter if it was a puma or a platypus. What mattered to him was its target: Gianna. It shoved her to the ground with its colossal paws, and the crack of her head colliding with the asphalt made his blood run cold.

Luke drew his handgun and pointed it at Lily. He no longer cared that the Dusk Walkers were not to be harmed. The puma whipped around, teeth bared at him. It was no cute kitty cat; this thing was hair-raising, and for Luke, that was not an image to be taken lightly.

Its wide brown eyes stared at the semiautomatic, challenging the weapon. He did not want to shoot the girl, but if she attacked him, he could easily claim her injury as self-defense. Lily appeared to have detected his hesitation when she moved, slowly at first, toward Jack. Fearing she might turn into some other animal and carry her friend away, Luke squeezed the trigger on his pistol and fired a single shot into the air. When that got the puma's attention, he aimed the gun at Jack.

The puma lifted its lip in anger, exposing its sharp teeth. Just as he was about to shoot again, the feline morphed into what looked like a raven grown to several times its natural size, and it soared toward him. He ducked just in time for it to fly over his head, and he turned around to see a sight that had changed since he had last looked. Rae slumped against the ledge of the roof, clutching the back of her head, and Eva carried Jack's knife and bag. The bird swooped close to her, growing rapidly in size, and the girl gripped onto the creature's feet.

Soon, they were flying off the roof, away from Luke. He could not shoot at them, which would only send the two Dusk Walkers plummeting to their deaths. He could only watch them escape, although he felt no sinking in his chest, nor any sense of disappointment. They had the oldest Dusk Walker, the only boy, the one whom everybody cared about the most. He rushed to help the injured and extended a hand to pull Rae to her feet. Blood trickled from her nose down her chin, and her hair rested in knots on top of her head. She moaned and leaned against his shoulder for a moment. "You gonna be all right?"

She nodded, smearing the blood across her lip with the back of her hand. "Yeah, I'm just…just a bit woozy."

"It's a good thing we've got ambulances on the way," said Luke. "D'you think they would come up here? It is a parking garage after all, and we've probably got press down there waiting to attack us as soon as we show our faces." He glanced over the ledge. There was, as he suspected, a small crowd of people surrounding the building. He saw at least three news vans.

"I'll call the dispatcher," said Rae. "You go check on Gianna."

He gave her a smile and a pat on the shoulder. She whipped out her radio, but he did not hear what she said. He rushed to Gianna's side instead, the skin on his knees breaking when he skidded across the jagged ground. She was awake, but her eyes were out of focus when she looked at him. Her eyelids drooped lazily and she furrowed her brows. "Was I in an accident?"

"A puma attacked you on the roof of a parking garage," said Luke. "Do you remember that?"

Gianna gawked at him, blinking slowly. "I think I'm concussed."

"The ambulances are coming any minute. They'll patch you up." They would arrive soon, and she would be hurried to the nearest hospital. He heard sirens approaching. Judging by the otherwise silent streets, they were a couple of blocks away.

"Luke?"

"Yeah?"

"The bag." She pointed to her duffel bag, which had been left at the entrance to the garage. "You'll have to give him the chip yourself."

"I don't know how, Gee."

"Then text me when you need it turned on. I can do it from a distance if I concentrate."

"Are you sure you can do that with a concussion?"

"Yeah. Just get him to swallow it."

Luke looked at Jack. "How am I supposed to do that? He's going to wake up any minute now."

"You'll come up with something." Gianna smiled and Luke frowned. He was not known for his creativity. He sighed heavily and ran his fingers through his hair, which had risen in his stress.

The ambulances arrived only moments later. Two gurneys, operated by one paramedic and one technician each, arrived on the scene. Luke stepped out of the way while Gianna was examined. He walked to the other patients. Rae refused an EMT's help into the second ambulance, only accepting a towel to sponge the worst of the blood from her face.

Jack was already on a gurney, the frame of the stretcher aligned almost perfectly with the white painted lines of the parking space. The paramedic in charge buckled the straps around Jack's chest, waist, and knees. Luke hurried to help lift the gurney to its regular height, for the EMT was busy inside the ambulance. As they wheeled the Dusk Walker toward the vehicle, Luke shot a glance at the boy. While he was horribly pale, he did not know if that was normal or not. Jack lay still, but Luke thought he caught a glimpse of bright blue from between Jack's eyelids.

"When will he wake up?" he asked the paramedic, a man of about thirty years with olive skin and a wide, sturdy jaw. The EMT inside the ambulance helped pull the gurney inside and locked it snugly into place.

"He's in electric shock," said the paramedic. They both climbed into the ambulance, Rae following suit. "It's tough to tell when he'll come out of it because of the abnormal source of the electricity mixed with his healing, but I doubt it'll be long now."

The EMT sat in the driver's seat, and the paramedic in the chair bolted to the wall behind the gurney. Luke and Rae slid onto the bench, Gianna's duffel bag between them. He prepared himself to open it, and then his phone buzzed in his jacket pocket. He frowned, because Gianna was a technopath and not a telepath, incapable of knowing that he was ready to open the bag.

The caller ID read, 'Captain Roy.' Luke's chest tightened in dread and he answered. "Warren."

"I know you're not gonna like this, but I need you to talk to the press."

"But—"

"I talked to Gianna. She said you got Turner. You need to let the public know that. It'll make you look good, trust me. It doesn't have to be a long speech. Just stop on your way out of the garage and hop out of the ambulance." Roy knew of his discomfort with journalists and cameras, so he would not have instructed Luke to speak to the public unless it was necessary.

"Thank you, Sir. We'll do it." He put the phone back into his pocket and exchanged glances with Rae, who still held the towel to her nose. "The blood will make you look good," said Luke, echoing Roy.

☢

Jack had the fleeting impression that he was going to be sick. He was moving now, moving through the air while still lying on his back. No, he had stopped. Earlier, he had felt buckles restraining him, but no more. Strange. He tasted blood inside of his mouth from when he had bitten his lip. Even though the cut had healed, the brackish taste lingered in his mouth. He swallowed, his head spinning in the process. His stomach turned over, and for a split second, he expected to throw up. He leaned his head to the side so he would not choke on his own vomit, but nothing came.

He remembered pieces of what had happened. After the shot of electricity, he had seen flashes of his surroundings: a paramedic's face, streetlamps from the rooftop. As for his current situation, he had no way of knowing if he was still in captivity of if he had escaped somehow. He thought of the other Dusk Walkers: Cordy, Eva, Lily, and Alix, and his mind gave a jolt. He could not doze off until he knew that his friends were safe. He returned to where he had previously been, at some point between awareness and not.

He took a deep breath, sending blood back to his extremities. He wiggled his fingers and toes. Although numb, they all worked. He lay flat on his back, his arms and legs straight. Through his reddened eyelids, he saw light. He was certainly not back at the shadowy subway station. With the hope that the Dusk Walkers had moved him elsewhere and that he would wake to the four of them nearby, he blinked one eye open.

With a deception that sent his heart leaping to his throat in fear, he realized where he was. He had never been to the place, but he had enough experience to know it. The only question was why he felt no movement. An ambulance would, in his mind, roll down the streets, hurdling along the insufferable potholes that littered the roads.

The blur of his eyesight sharpening into something similar to focus, he turned from the ceiling of the ambulance to his right and saw shelves packed neatly with medical supplies, ranging from boxes of medications to gauze pads. A sunflower-yellow holding rail was near the roof, under cabinets that probably contained more equipment. He stirred, already feeling the symptoms of electric shock dissipating.

He heard, as though from a mile away, muffled voices. Several of them. They could not all be inside the ambulance. They were outside. That was why the vehicle was not moving. He strained to make sense of what the people said.

"Excuse me! Excuse me, Detective?" called the high-pitched voice of a woman. "Have you caught any of the other Dusk Walkers?"

"Where is Gianna Rossi?" Someone else spoke, a male.

"Why did one ambulance leave so quickly?"

"Why were there two ambulances in the first place? Did you plan on there being injuries?"

"Look," interrupted a calmer voice. Luke. "We'll try to answer your questions another time, but right now, we've got to finish our job. That's what you want us to do, right? Take Jack Turner in, protect the city?" A brief silence followed before he continued. "Well, we can't do that if we're answering your questions. Now could you please clear off so we can get this ambulance moving?"

No one spoke after that, so Jack assumed that the reporters had listened. If his hunch was correct, Luke and Rae would return to the ambulance at any moment. He sat up, not willing to greet his enemies lying down on a gurney. Blood churning inside his head like in a half-empty bowl, he groaned sharply and pressed the heel of his palm to his temple.

Something brushed against his shoulder and he nearly leapt out of his skin. He whirled around, his heartbeat racing out of his chest. A man sat on the seat behind the gurney, clothed in a navy-blue uniform. Jack saw a paramedic badge on the front of the man's shirt.

"Careful, boy," said the man. "You're experiencing the symptoms of severe electric shock. Tell me, do you feel any nausea, confusion, numbness, trouble breathing, or memory loss?"

Jack paused, weighing each of the symptoms. He felt fine now, despite his previous soreness. "Nope."

Now the paramedic was confused, his mouth open in awe. Jack thought about the amount of electricity he had received from Luke, enough to render him unconscious. He deduced that most people did not recover as quickly as he had.

As much as the paramedic's surprise was amusing, Jack needed to get out of the ambulance before the Hunters returned. He looked at the exit. Luke would be there, and Jack could not outrun him. He was faced with two choices, and neither of them was desirable: He could stay in the ambulance and wait to be escorted elsewhere, or he could run outside in the hope that everyone's backs would be turned.

Where was his knife? He patted his pockets and belt, as though it hid from him there. He knew perfectly well that it was gone because its familiar weight was absent. And Eva. Where was she? He cursed himself for forgetting her for even a moment. She was obviously not in the ambulance, so she had to be elsewhere. He made his decision.

The paramedic leapt to his feet at the same time as Jack. "Don't go out there!"

He glanced back and scoffed, blood boiling. No one would tell him what to do. Not the Nor'easters, not Luke, and certainly not this stupid man. Jack turned toward the doors and stepped up to the yellow caution line painted into the metal floor. He reached for the handles, but the doors swung open before he even touched them.

Jack flinched back, stumbling over his feet as he did so. There was nothing good for him toward the back of the ambulance, but he still retreated from Luke and Rae.

"Sit down," said Luke in a disinterested tone. Behind him, Rae closed the doors and slid onto the bench.

Jack did not budge. He merely stared up at Luke, who

was at least half a foot taller than him, and tried not to blink. The detective did not take the contest so seriously. He scoffed. Jack blinked. When he opened his eyes, a cold metal band cut into his wrist.

As he stared at the handcuffs, understanding that Luke had put them there in a fraction of a second, the Hunter pushed him backward until his thighs bumped against the gurney. "Sit," said Luke more forcefully this time. His eyebrows, half-hidden by his wild hair, curved with his mouth in a mocking smile. "Please?"

Jack had no choice. He was easily comparable to a grudgingly obedient dog when he climbed back onto the gurney. Luke secured Jack's wrist to the handlebar of the gurney, leaving his right hand, the one against the ambulance's wall, free.

"Roll up your sleeve."

Jack frowned and began to shake his head. Then under the hard command of Luke's eyes alone, Jack rolled up the sleeve of his sweater past his elbow.

"Was that so difficult?" Luke gripped the handlebar, leaning closer to Jack. He felt a chill shiver down his spine and averted his gaze from those grey eyes. He glanced at Rae, whose nose was no longer bloody. She sat with her leg draped nonchalantly over the other. When she saw him looking, she turned her silky blond head toward the paramedic. She nodded, and the man in the uniform crouched in front of a cabinet.

Jack followed the paramedic with his eyes, wondering just what exactly he was searching for, what he had known to retrieve after just a nod from Rae. He would not know until later. Luke took advantage of Jack's brief distraction to push against his chest with two fingers until Jack lay down.

"Good boy." Luke took something the paramedic handed him. A loaded syringe. Jack immediately sat up, but was shoved back down. He reached over with his free hand in an effort to hit the syringe to the ground, but Luke's fingers wrapped tightly around his wrist, and with the same hand he pushed down on Jack's chest so he could not get up.

The point of the needle pinched his exposed forearm, and his muscles contracted. He did not move, frozen as he anticipated the anesthetic's effect. He tried to keep his eyes open, but they were so heavy. He did not know if Luke had pulled out the needle. He could not feel his arm.

His eyes closed, and he knew no more.

CHAPTER SEVEN

Light blinded Jack, and he tried his best not to turn away. Luke would probably put his electricity back to use if he did not cooperate. The doctor lowered his flashlight, and Jack blinked rapidly to rid his eyes of the spots in his sight. The interrogation room around him came into focus. The white-going-on-beige walls reflected the light from the florescent lamps on the ceiling. He almost lifted his right hand to rub his eyes before he remembered that he was handcuffed to a hook on the table in front of him. His left hand did the job as the doctor took notes on his clipboard.

"Stand on the scale, please," said the white-haired man. Beads of sweat pooled at the elder's receding hairline, and his possession of five chins was fascinating. Jack was grateful that the doctor wore latex gloves.

He pushed the chair away so that the medical scale could be moved closer to him. He shot Luke a careful glance to ask if the examination could end already. The doctor had claimed it would last two seconds, but ten minutes had passed, and Jack was still poked and prodded. After he had woken up in the ambulance, he had been guided straight to the police station and into interview room four, where a fat man in a white coat awaited them.

Luke stood in his corner, and his hand rested on his gun holster. When Jack looked to him, he gave the smallest shake of his head, just enough to make himself clear. The doctor was to stay.

With a frown, Jack complied with the doctor's orders. It would be silly to make a big deal out of stepping onto a scale. He stood as straight as he could with his wrist still restrained to the table. The doctor adjusted the rulers, then lifted his clipboard to copy the information.

"Sixty-eight inches." His breath stank of old socks. "One hundred and twenty-seven pounds. You can sit back down now."

Jack pulled the chair to the table, leaning back and sighing heavily. He would much prefer to be questioned than to sit through the examination. The doctor moved the scale away and snapped open his briefcase that was on the table.

"Could I take a blood sample?" he asked Luke. "Just a small prick would suffice."

"As long as you send the results to my captain or to me as soon as you have them."

"Of course." The doctor fiddled with some objects inside of his briefcase, which smelled just too clean. He emerged with a drawing needle. Jack wrinkled his nose, far from eager to be stabbed with one of those again. After cleaning the patch of skin above his vein with an alcoholic wipe, the doctor took Jack's right arm and pricked his forearm, extracting a small amount of blood. Before replacing his equipment, the doctor peered at the speck of scarlet on Jack's arm, his cool latex gloves still around Jack's wrist. The spot of blood slowly shrank back into the puncture wound, and then there was no sign of it. "Incredible," said the doctor, still staring. Jack fidgeted in his chair.

"Is that all?" said Luke. "I have work to do."

The fat man nodded eagerly. "Yes, yes, yes...of course, Detective. Thank you for letting me come." He gathered his things and hurried out the door on the left. As soon as he was gone, Jack spoke.

"I don't like him."

"Don't judge him. He's fascinated with you, that's all. You just don't like him because he was staring." Luke came to sit across from Jack. He placed a cell phone on the table between them, not appearing to have it out for any particular purpose. He merely twirled it on the flat surface, stroking the fingerprint-smeared screen with his thumb.

Jack watched for what seemed like the longest time. He had expected to be questioned about the locations of the other Dusk Walkers. Since he did not know the answer, perhaps he could stall the cops for as long as he could. Cordy, Eva, Lily, and Alix were coming for him, surely. It was only a matter of time before they arrived. He glanced uncertainly at the camera on the tripod near the one-way mirror. There was no sign that it was on, but he did not doubt that his interrogation would be recorded and analyzed in detail.

The door opened, and a man entered the room, sporting a very hairy mustache and very bald head. Jack thought he could be in his late forties. This man was not a Hunter. There were only three of those.

"Jack Turner." The stranger's voice was deep, but smooth. He had heard it somewhere, but not in person. "We meet at last."

"I guess you aren't as famous as I am. I don't know who you are."

"Captain Stanley Roy. I'm going to be asking you a few questions."

He immediately recognized the name from the radio. "Right...you're the guy who does all those interviews." Roy was the Hunters' superior, who regularly warned the city that the Dusk Walkers were extremely dangerous and not to be approached. The citizens of New York obeyed that caution, for the most part.

"Among other things, but yes, that is what I do," said Roy. Luke picked up his phone and left his chair, and the captain sat down, placing a manila folder on the table. "But we're not here to talk about me. We're here to talk about you. Have you been informed of your rights?"

Jack nodded. Luke had read them to him in the ambulance before they arrived.

"Then let's get started. Is your name Jackson Dean Turner?"

The first query was not what Jack had expected. He

shifted his gaze once more to Luke, who had returned to his spot in the corner of the room. He, too, seemed confused. Jack nodded at Roy. "Yeah."

"How do you know that's your name?"

Jack narrowed his eyes as he thought. What did Roy expect him to say? He risked the truth. "I saw it on missing posters with my picture three years ago. Not long after that, they became wanted posters."

"Ah..." Roy liked that answer. "And on those posters, what are you wanted for?"

"My good looks?" Jack shrugged. A lie. He knew exactly what was written.

Roy shook his head, not liking that answer. He opened the folder and withdrew a copy of a wanted poster identical to the one Jack had seen on his way to visit the Nor'easters. Roy pointed at a series of bold black letters near the top. "Read that for me."

Jack did not need to read anything. He had seen the poster enough times already. "Jack Turner: wanted for robbery, vandalism, assault, and breaking and entering."

"Do you deny any of those?"

"No."

"No?" repeated Roy, his forehead creased in surprise. "Do you deny the injuries you inflicted on Samuel Jensen?"

"Who?"

"He's the police officer who you attacked and threatened on the rooftop of the parking garage a few hours ago."

"Oh…" Jack sucked his teeth. "No, I'm not denying it."

Roy stood and stared down at Jack. He did not have the choice but to return the stare. "He was an innocent man, and he was put in the hospital because of you."

"Then I'll be sure to send him a get-well card."

"Enough with the wisecracks, kid," said Luke.

"Eat me." Jack's lip raised in a snarl, and he barely turned his head to speak. Luke glared back. The rest of his face remained hard as a statue.

Roy cleared his throat. "Next question: What do you remember from the power-plant meltdown that occurred three years ago?"

"Nothing." It was an easy question, but Roy was determined to find another answer.

"Nothing? Not a single face or event?"

"No. That's my final answer."

"Are you sure?"

"What is so hard to understand about 'no'?"

Roy raised his hands in mocking surrender. "Okay. I can see that this is a difficult subject for you. Let's try a different approach."

Jack rolled his eyes. It was not a difficult subject, only an annoying one. How could he have possibly forgotten the first fourteen years of his life? It was often the cause of long, sleepless days where he spent hours with his eyes closed, wondering about those lost years. Had he been as obnoxious as he was now, or had he been sweet and innocent? Did he have a brother? A sister? A goldfish? He sometimes imagined a different life for himself, one where he lived behind a white picket fence and where his parents welcomed him home every day after school. Occasionally he would give himself a dog or two, or a friendly neighbor. He could imagine that life without much hesitation, but it was impossible to put his own face in the place of the lucky boy.

He dragged himself back to the world where he really lived, the only life he knew. It was his only reality. He could not see himself anywhere other than in the truth where he and his friends were hunted by the government and feared by everyone. That was how things were, and they could never change.

Roy pulled out the remaining contents of the folder: a printed document and three photos. He slid the paper across the table.

"Not the happiest childhood. Go on, read it."

Jack reluctantly leaned forward. He had wanted answers for three years, and many of them were right in front of him. All he had to do was look. And that was exactly what he did. He skimmed the page to read that he was born asthmatic, but was otherwise a happy child, with two loving parents and a roof over his head until he was seven. His mother, Erin Turner, had been diagnosed with breast cancer. The next year she passed away, and his father Gabriel grew fond of drinking himself to sleep. It soon became an addiction, and he took his drunken misery out on his son. This went on until Jack was fourteen. The beatings became too much for him, and the asthma attack that ensued put him in the hospital for several days. Gabriel confessed to hitting his son upon the discovery of Jack's injuries, and he was sentenced to one year in prison. Meanwhile, Jack was sent to a children's shelter, having no relatives willing to accept him into their home. Then on the night of November second, the Explosion devastated the city, and Jack was nowhere to be found.

He looked up. Roy had been watching him carefully.

"That's a sad story. Too bad I don't remember a thing." Jack had expected to read that he had been normal or happy. It was the opposite. He had never been anything but miserable, except for when he was a small child. It was hardly much comfort.

The police captain nodded, then placed two of the three pictures on top of the document, not showing him the other. The first was a class photo. A small girl held up a black square that read 'Mrs. Keeney, class 102'. Jack cast a quick look at the faces, all of them too happy for him to bear at the moment. None of the children were any older than seven years old. The teacher on the left was tall and brooding, and she appeared as though she had just been punched in the face. And where was he? Jack searched for a younger version of himself among the strange kids. He had to be there somewhere, or Roy would have had no reason to show him the picture. There he was!

He did not make a point of observing himself in a mirror very often, but he and the boy in the picture shared the same flop of auburn hair. The younger boy's bone structure was not dissimilar from Jack's, except the seven-year-old was rounder. He felt goose bumps on his arms. He knew this picture. He knew the girl who stood in front of him. The tag of her flowered cardigan had been visible on her neck. He could picture Mrs. Keeney, who had been as icy as ever that day. Out of the corner of his eye, he saw her standing on his right. Her fists were clenched at her side. Jack could see the metal bench under his feet, not from the photographer's point of view but from his own. Jack remembered.

He withdrew his hands from the photo as though it were aflame. This had never happened to him before. Once, years ago, Alix had ventured to mention a vivid dream that she had when she was half-asleep. She had said that it felt like *déjà vu*. Jack had not believed her at first, and in his jealousy he had told her not to mention her flashbacks again. However, as he experienced the same thing, he understood. His vision of the girl's tag and of Mrs. Keeney's fists no longer felt surreal. He knew, somehow, that it had all happened. He had only forgotten.

Jack cleared his throat and moved onto the second picture, which was smaller than the first. A family of three, clothed in red and white, stood in front of a fireplace. The mantel was covered in silvery tinsel and miniature fake wreaths. Sitting in front of the silent fire were an auburn-haired, doe-eyed woman in her thirties, a fat man with a fat nose, and a young boy, clearly the biological child of the adults who embraced him. It was the same boy from the other picture: Jack.

"Still nothing?" said Roy once Jack looked up. "No *déjà vu* vibes?"

The hairs on the back of his neck raised straight into the air at the captain's choice of words. It was only a coincidence, he told himself. It was a common expression. Roy had not seen Jack's reaction to the pictures. Roy had not read his mind. Jack shook his head and sneaked another glimpse at the picture of the family. He recognized his own auburn hair and straight nose from the woman. His mom. His blue eyes and crescent-shaped eyebrows seemed to come from his father.

Another photo landed on top of it.

"How about this one?"

It was a headshot of Jack, from just before the Explosion, because he had not aged since then due to his healing powers. In the picture, he did not smile. In fact, he did not look happy at all. His lip was split, and his left cheek was swollen and red. Jack swallowed hard. He experienced no *déjà vu*. He did not know when or how the picture was taken, but he remembered the exact same injuries.

It was his first memory, the night of the Explosion. He had woken up in a bed—now he knew that it was in the children's shelter—and when he had run to the bathroom to vomit, he had looked in the mirror. As he stared on in shock, the same split lip and bruised cheek had healed at a superhuman speed.

Tremendously confused at the events that were taking place, he had run. Then a few blocks away from the building he had come across a young, crying girl with short dark hair: Cordy. Afterward they had found the other strange children with powers, and they had become the Dusk Walkers. Their group name had originated in a newspaper report. The journalist writing the article had come up with the phrase, and it had been theirs ever since.

"Well?" said Roy.

Before replying, Jack wiped away all signs of having remembered that night and the bruises induced by his cruel father. "No. I don't remember anything. Why are you asking these questions?"

A knock on the door alerted Roy before he could answer. The captain spun around and let in a slim officer with a gaunt face. "Captain? Chief Riley wants to speak to you."

"Can't it wait? I'm in the middle of an interview," said Roy.

"He said it's urgent, Sir."

Jack lifted the corner of his lip in a slow half-smile when Roy looked at him. "Tell the chief I'll be with him in just a minute," said the captain. The officer nodded and left the room. Roy turned to Luke. "You gonna be okay?"

The Hunter nodded. Roy's thick moustache twitched, and Jack thought it might be a smile. Roy took long strides out of the room, the door snapping shut behind him. Luke came to lean against the table and pulled the phone out of his pocket once again. He held down a button and brought it to his ear.

"Who're you calling?" said Jack, rubbing his wrist where the handcuffs were tight.

"It's none of your business."

"Oh, come on. Who do you have on speed-dial? Got a girl? Got a guy?"

Luke shook his head, then began to speak into the phone. "Hey. Heard anything?" He kept his voice low, as though that would prevent Jack from hearing. "All right. Tell me when you have news…okay, bye." He pocketed the phone and ran his fingers through his wild hair nervously.

"What is it?"

"No one was talking to you."

"Is someone hurt?" Jack tugged on his jacket zipper while watching Luke's apprehensive face. Then the answer dawned on him. "It's Gianna, isn't it? She was hurt, and that's why there were two ambulances."

Luke clenched his jaw, which Jack took for a yes.

"And in the ambulance, only Rae was there, because Gianna couldn't come—"

"She was hurt on the roof," snapped the Hunter. "What does it matter to you?"

"Was that Rae on the phone? Is she at the hospital?"

"Maybe."

"Are you and Gianna together?" Luke stared at him, his expression a cross between confusion and pissed-off. "You are, aren't you?" Jack grinned.

Luke did not answer, instead scowling at him before leaving. Jack would have to remember to congratulate whichever of his companions had hurt Gianna, for it had rendered Luke speechless.

"Touchy," said Jack to the door once it had closed behind the Hunter.

CHAPTER EIGHT

Luke sat at his desk on the second floor of the police station, typing away at his computer. His job had its benefits, but sitting still for long periods of time was definitely not one of them. Roy was still in Chief Riley's office, and Rae had not left the hospital. Once Jack had been delivered to the station, she had ridden in the ambulance to visit Gianna. According to Rae, Gianna was awake, but had gone back to sleep before she could speak to her.

While his colleagues were occupied, Luke had ordered for Jack to be placed in a holding cell until someone could continue the interview. Since Roy had told him nothing of their interrogation strategy, Luke could not ask any questions of Jack. He would have gone to visit Gianna, but Roy needed him to write the report on the events of that night. Luke glanced at his watch. It was two o'clock in the morning. It was no wonder that he could hardly concentrate. He gritted his teeth and returned to his computer. When he finished he would get himself a nice cup of coffee or three.

He had already filled out the easy information: Jack's full name, lack of address, and birth date. He had made note of all the officers involved, along with the names of each of the Dusk Walkers. Now he only had to complete the details of arrest, which required him to think. He dug the heel of his palm into his eye and rubbed vigorously.

"Detective Warren?" A harried-looking officer stood in front of his desk. Luke could not remember seeing him anywhere before. Then again, this was the night crew. On most nights, Luke was asleep.

"Yes?"

"Captain Roy is out of his meeting. He told me to tell you to get Turner and to bring him to interview room four."

"Okay, sure," said Luke. He turned off the monitor on his computer and crossed the area toward the holding cells. Indoors he tried to avoid putting on bursts of speed so that he would not run into anyone in his path. The precinct was a busy one that night, full of staff members bustling about with their papers and camera feeds.

When he arrived at Jack's cell, the officer who stood in front of the unit glanced at Luke once, but did not linger after handing him a set of keys. The young prisoner lay on the small cot at the far side of the cell, staring at the ceiling. Luke tapped on one of the metal bars to get Jack's attention.

"Come on, kid, let's go." He turned the key in the lock and pulled the door open.

"Where?"

"Back to where you just came from," said Luke. Jack

crossed his arms over his chest. Luke snapped his fingers to regain his attention. "Hey! Get over here."

Jack curved his head back around and blinked, obviously taking his time to decide whether to get up or not. It was not hard to see that he did not like being told what to do. Neither did Luke, for that matter. Finally, Jack groaned and rolled off the bed before standing up straight. Luke secured handcuffs around his wrists, quickly putting a finger between Jack's skin and the cuff to ensure it was not too tight. Luke then led him past the other jeering prisoners, up the stairs, and in the direction of the interview room. A number of curious heads stopped their work and turned their way. Jack walked along silently, much to Luke's surprise.

"You're quiet."

"Did you want me to say anything?"

"No, it's just unusual." Luke doubted that Jack would try to run away, which was what he had initially expected. They were surrounded by many armed officers who would surely shoot the boy before he could escape, if Luke would have not already done the job.

"It's just...unusual," repeated Jack, mockery heavy in his voice.

"Forget it, we're here." Luke put a hand on the other's shoulder to stop him. The door to the interview room was not going to be easy to get past. Two officers stood before them. "Hey, guys, mind letting us through?"

"Captain Roy wants to conduct the interview himself.

He said for you to wait in the observation room, Warren," said the one with a slack face and hooded eyes.

Luke frowned. Perhaps this was because of how he had nearly throttled Jack only an hour ago. He had not allowed the boy the chance to insult Gianna, but if he had, Luke's fist would have collided with Jack's face hard enough to knock him out of the chair. However, that had not happened. Luke had done the right thing and restrained himself. So why was he excluded from the interview?

"Fine. I'll leave him with you, then."

The officers guided Jack inside and reattached the handcuffs to the table that faced the mirror. Luke closed the door, turning toward the observation room. He made the slightest flinch of surprise when he saw Roy only steps before him.

"Captain, they said you wouldn't let me in. Why—" He froze. His superior was haggard, his posture unusually rigid. Roy pushed up his white sleeves with trembling fingers. His eyes darted around, not focusing on anything. "Sir, what's wrong?"

For the first time that Luke knew, Roy was restless. He continued to fidget with his sleeve and would not look anywhere but at his feet. "The hospital contacted Chief Riley."

Horror sliced through Luke, settling in his heart and causing his mind to leap to rapid conclusions. Gianna was in trouble. There had been an accident. She was dying, or worse. She was the first Hunter, the first that Roy had found. She had practically forced Luke to take the position as the team leader in her place. Now something had happened to her. That was why Roy was so distressed.

The captain cleared his throat. "My daughter Vanessa was just attacked."

Oh, thank God, thought Luke. Gianna was all right, as far as he knew. He then felt awful for wishing harm on Vanessa. He had met Roy's daughter once, at a Christmas party. She was only a few years younger than Luke, but she had kept her childhood spirit. She liked horses, he remembered. She majored in biology at a nearby university. He cleared his throat. "What happened to her? Was it the Dusk Walkers?"

"She was mugged and beaten, but she is still unconscious." As he said the words aloud, the police captain seemed to relax. His shoulders slacked, and his moustache twitched in a brief smile. "They can't be sure if it was the Dusk Walkers or not. I suppose they'll know when she wakes up."

"Why don't you go visit her? I'll take over here."

Roy shook his head. "I don't want you accidentally murdering Turner if he insults your girlfriend. I saw the tapes."

"I won't murder him! Besides, we can get Rae to come back if you want. She's got a level head."

"I want to be the one asking the questions. That's another reason I don't want you in there. I won't use the same angle you would."

"What d'you mean?"

"I don't want Turner to tell us where the other Dusk Walkers are," said Roy, his expression dark once more. "His arrest is all over the news. It isn't hard to figure out where we are. His friends will come for him. I just want to know if they hurt my daughter, and he can give me the answer."

"Sir, I don't know if that's a good idea…"

"I need to know, Warren. If you didn't know who had hurt Gianna, would you have fought to find her attacker?"

Luke did not have to think. He nodded. Roy walked briskly past him and into the interview room. Luke swallowed hard and entered the observation room. A lonely desk sat in the corner, hosting the camera feeds from the other side of the one-way mirror. He took a seat in the chair as Roy circled Jack's table. The captain drew a wallet from his back pocket. He held a photograph in front of the boy. Luke squinted and recognized Vanessa. "Do you know her?"

"No…" said Jack. He was hesitant to answer. Almost too hesitant, thought Luke. Perhaps he knew something.

"Do any of your friends know her?" Luke no longer understood Roy's approach. He would try to get answers out of Jack, but the Dusk Walker had been unconscious when Vanessa was attacked.

"If I don't know her, how would I know if anyone else knows her?" said Jack. That was a perfectly valid answer, thought Luke.

"This is my daughter."

"Oh." Jack took a closer look at the picture. "She's cute. Sort of."

"She was attacked just after you were arrested!"

Jack blinked slowly. "Okay…so there's my alibi. I couldn't have hurt her." Another valid answer.

"No, I don't think you did."

It only took a moment for Jack to understand. When he did, he straightened in his chair. "Wait, you don't think that the other Dusk Walkers did it?"

"That's exactly what I think."

"But they wouldn't—" He stopped before he could finish.

"They wouldn't? Why don't you say that to Sandy Collins and Michael Parsons, the patrolmen who Eva Edwards knocked out mercilessly only hours ago? Or say it to that nice old lady, Bella Morgan, who was also injured when you broke into her house last month?"

Jack's mouth fell open. He spoke in a whisper that barely registered on the recording. "Eva wouldn't hurt your daughter."

"Why not? She doesn't seem to have any trouble hurting other people." In Jack's silence, Roy leaned closer to him to appear more threatening. "I just arrested you. In spite, she tracked down my daughter and beat her up on the streets. This Eva character seems quite pretty. You're sufficiently good-looking for your age. Maybe she likes you enough to do something like that."

Jack shook his head. Through the glass, Luke noticed that his fists were clenched on the table to the point where his knuckles were white. "That's stupid. She wouldn't do that. It wouldn't get her anywhere. Why can't you just accept that some random guys on the street mugged your daughter? This happening now was just a coincidence. It doesn't have anything to do with me or Ev!"

Luke watched both of their faces carefully. Roy was convinced that the Dusk Walkers were the ones who had hurt Vanessa, and Jack was determined that they were not the wrongdoers. But only one of them was right.

The door to the observation room opened, but Luke did not pay attention. He only had eyes for what was on the other side of the glass.

"Luke?" said Rae. "Gianna's fine, she's at your place with M-G. Brought you some coffee—"

"Shh!" he whispered as he did when he watched football on television, which sometimes annoyed Gianna so much that she shut it off with a snap of her fingers.

Rae placed the coffee on the desk and looked through the mirror. "What's going on?"

"Roy's daughter was just attacked. Vanessa, remember her? He thinks that it was the Dusk Walkers."

"What do you think?"

Luke shook his head. "I don't think it was them."

In the interview room, Roy shook his head in defeat before he walked out the door. He arrived momentarily in the observation room.

"Captain, I think he's right."

"Excuse me?"

"The Dusk Walkers have no reason to hurt Vanessa. Like Jack said, it wouldn't get them anywhere except for jail once they're caught. Also, I think he knows where they're hiding. If we can't get him to confess about Vanessa, we can at least try to get a location on the other kids before they hurt anyone else."

"Really?" Roy looked apprehensive. He knew what Luke would say next.

"I think I could try to get him to talk."

Roy narrowed his eyes. "How exactly do you plan to do that?"

"I'll try the power of love first. And if that doesn't work, I'll use what little logic I have. Just like a real cop, right?" said Luke. The captain stroked his moustache in deep thought, and then nodded. Luke smiled and headed toward the door. "Thanks, Captain."

He dropped the smile as soon as he left the observation room. He would have to focus during the interview. He had very little police training to account for, and most of it consisted of manipulating a pistol. But he had still learned how to conduct an interview. He took a deep breath. He would be fine, and he would prove himself to be a worthy imitation of a cop. He gripped the doorknob and pushed before he could have another thought.

CHAPTER NINE

Luke could tell that Jack was tired. He showed no obvious signs of exhaustion such as rubbing his eyes or yawning, but the lazy way he blinked and his abnormal silence were enough. Luke cleared his throat.

"You know, you aren't leaving this room until you tell me where the other Dusk Walkers are."

"Guess we've got a long night ahead of us, then."

"It's nearly dawn."

Jack's eyebrows shot up in surprise. He stared at the table in silence. Despite his fatigue, the young criminal did not relent. Luke sat down and leaned forward, wearing the most serious expression he could manage.

"No one's gonna come save you. Your only way to take a break or eat or sleep is to give me this information. Just one tiny location. I'm sure your friends will understand, and they won't be mad at you. If you tell me, you'll get to stay with them. If not, you rot here alone. Your choice." Luke thought he had done a pretty good job. Jack did not agree.

"Nah. Even if I tell you, and you manage to bring

them all here safe and sound, we're still going to rot in jail, right? Unless you decide to kill us off." He had a point, but Luke did not let that show. Jack licked his lips and lowered his voice. "And did you ever consider the fact that once they kill us off, you're next? Those jerks used you to hunt us down. So what happens once I'm gone?"

"I've heard nothing about killing the Dusk Walkers. Anyway, have you considered the possibility that I could help arrest other criminals? I'd be doing a lot for the city that way, and they wouldn't have to kill me, Gianna, and Rae."

Jack shook his head. "They're scared of you too, you know. They're afraid you'll turn against them or something. So once I'm out of the picture, the famous Hunters will be—" He swept his index finger across his throat from left to right. "Think about that."

"How can you be sure that the New York government is made up of a bunch of sadistic bastards who'll kill anyone who's a threat to society?"

"Because I'm a very good example. The New York government wants to kill me because I'm a threat to society. Therefore, they are sadistic bastards. I win."

The door to the interview room opened and Roy entered, accompanied by Rae and the two officers who had stood in front of the door earlier.

"Change of plans, Turner. You're going back to your cell," said Roy. The officers pulled Jack to his feet, and the captain turned to Luke. "You did great, but we've got to cut this short."

"I was right," said Jack. "They would only stop this if I was saying the truth. Oh, and Captain? Your daughter was mugged. Check for her wallet or anything valuable that she carries around."

Luke stood as soon as Jack was led out the door. It took his full power not to appear angry. "Sir, I wasn't even getting started. Why did you interfere?"

Roy did not answer the question directly. He did not even meet Luke's eyes. "You don't believe him about the Hunters being next in line for the gallows, do you?"

"No, of course not." He knew that Jack was right about more than he probably thought he was. Roy had already told Luke that when the Dusk Walkers were all arrested, the children would have to be put down to prevent them from escaping and wreaking more havoc. Luke could only wonder about what Jack had said about the Hunters meeting the same fate. It was more than possible.

"Warren," said Roy. "Do you want to go home and rest? You can see if Rossi is feeling any better."

Luke forgot all thoughts of being murdered, and he grinned. "Really? You'd let me?"

"I want you back before four o'clock, and I want your full report by midnight, but yes. You can go home." He addressed Rae. "Anderson, you'll stay here until Warren comes back, then you can get some rest. I can't have you two passing out on the job."

"Thank you, Sir."

"Thanks so much."

Roy decided that there were too many positive feelings in the room. "All right, get out. Lieutenant Rosenthal need this place in ten minutes."

Luke and Rae exchanged smiles before heading out the door. Roy marched in the direction of the holding cells, his head held high.

"Rae, keep an eye on the captain for me. And if you can, get him to visit his daughter in the hospital."

"I will. See you later." She turned to follow Roy while Luke gathered his coat and keys. His papers could stay there. He was not planning on working when he got home. He hurried onto the street and prepared to run back to his apartment as fast as he could. His plan was ruined when he caught sight of what awaited him outside.

"Detective!" A woman in a rosy trench coat thrust a recording device under his chin before he could pretend to not see her. The sinking feeling of dread bore a hole in his gut while he grimaced.

Purple bags under the reporter's eyes indicated that she had been awake for the better part of the night. Her nose and cheeks were pink from the chill, although she donned an air of excitement when she spotted him.

"I'm Holly Rose McBride. Can I have a word?"

"Sure." Luke did not hide his scowl. She prevented

him from getting back to Gianna. "I thought all of the reporters had been sent away hours ago."

Holly Rose McBride smiled, her chapped lips stretched. "Well, not us. Matt and I thought to stick around to hear the story first. Have you started searching for the other Dusk Walkers?"

Matt, a broad-shouldered man in a leather jacket, hoisted a large camera contraption onto his shoulder. Luke blinked at him briefly, worrying suddenly about his own physical state. He had not slept in ages. He had been on his feet all day. He probably looked awful.

"As soon as Jack Turner reveals where they are, my team and I will make finding them a priority." Luke remembered what Roy said about waiting for the Dusk Walkers instead of searching for them, but the public did not have to know.

After he left the reporter and the cameraman, it only took ten seconds for Luke to reach his apartment. In his hurry, he got turned around somewhere after the parkway before finding the correct trail home. He unlocked the front door of the building, then raced up the stairs to the third floor. The elevator was too slow for him.

Luke stopped in front of apartment 304 and opened the door. He glanced from the kitchen on the right to the sitting area in the back. No one was there. He closed the door behind him and continued into the bedroom. Gianna slept in their bed, and Marial Grace sat in an armchair reading a book. When she saw him, she stood, and they left the room so that they could speak without disturbing Gianna.

"Happy belated birthday," said M-G. "I wasn't expecting you until a lot later."

"Roy's feeling generous all of a sudden. Rae and I will switch places around four o'clock."

"Okay—" Her cell phone rang, and she pulled it out of her pocket to check. "Ugh, I've got to go. They need me back at the lab. Gianna's resting, but she's feeling better."

"Thanks, M-G."

"No problem. Oh, and she told me to give you this if you came while she was sleeping." She took a small envelope from her jacket pocket and handed it to him before letting herself out of the apartment.

Luke did not want to wake Gianna, so he sat on the couch, leaning back against the cushions and putting his feet on the coffee table. Oh, it felt so good to finally sit in a comfortable place. Quickly breaking the seal on the envelope, he discovered a folded sheet of paper and spread it out on his leg. It was an eight-by-eleven-inch printing paper that was blank on one side. He turned it over. Two words were inscribed in Gianna's slanted calligraphy: 'I'm pregnant.'

Luke dropped the paper. He had read that wrong; it couldn't be true. When he picked it back up, the words were still there, clear as day. Gianna was carrying his child.

When his heart finally stopped racing, he took a deep breath and considered the news. A baby was unexpected, but definitely not impossible. Just over a month ago they had not used protection. They had been aware of the potential consequences, but he had never imagined that Gianna would actually get pregnant. He wanted to wake her up now, to talk to her. He could not wait.

He had no choice but to return to the bedroom. Gianna was still fast asleep on her side of the bed. Luke shrugged off his coat and threw it onto the armchair where M-G had sat before. He climbed onto the edge of the mattress and pushed Gianna's hair away from her face. Her eyebrows furrowed and her fingers curled on the white sheets that she slept under.

"Hey, Gee…it's me," he whispered loud enough for her to hear in her subconsciousness.

She slowly opened her eyes. It took a moment for her to realize who he was, then she grinned. "Hi, there."

"How're you feeling?"

"Been better. I'm concussed."

"So I hear. Tell me if you need anything."

"I will."

"Okay. Oh, and M-G gave me this." Luke smiled nervously, then held up the note with the two words. Gianna swallowed hard and spoke in a whisper.

"What do you want to do?"

"I really don't know." Luke put the paper down and

took her hand in his. "I'll be honest with you: I'm not ready to be a dad. Maybe in a few months, I will be. Whatever you want to do, I'll support you, and I'll take care of you. No matter what it takes."

"Right back at you." Her eyes, reflecting the light of the table lamp, sparkled with tears. She did not speak for almost a minute. He let her. "I want to keep it. It won't be easy with a life like ours, but it'll be worth it in the end."

"Yeah, it will be."

How would the government react? Would they force Gianna to go through tests and experiments, since it would be the child of two superbeings? Would they leave them alone?

"Hey," said Luke. "What would the radiation do to the kid? We were both exposed and affected, so something could happen, right?"

"Since I wasn't exposed while pregnant, the baby shouldn't be too badly marked. At least, that's what M-G said. It's hard to tell."

"And what about the concussion?"

She shook her head, then grimaced at the movement. "It's way too early in the pregnancy for anything to happen."

He could not stop himself from grinning. Things were starting to look up. Jack Turner was caught, Gianna was okay, and… "We're going to be parents," he said before kissing her.

CHAPTER TEN

The quickened pace of Luke's footsteps, boot on concrete, alerted Jack of the Hunter's arrival.

"Hi," said Rae. Her chair creaked as she stood. The sound of her shoes clicked for a few steps, lighter than Luke's. "You're back earlier than I expected."

"And glad to be. You look exhausted."

Jack imagined that Rae had an expression of denial on her face, since he could not see her. He lay on his side, facing the back wall of the cell. His eyes were closed to better listen to the sounds around him. He had been asleep from the time Luke had left to when he returned, but now Jack only faked slumber in order to listen to the conversation that took place outside of the cell.

"So…" said Rae. "Did Gianna tell you—"

"Yeah, she told me," said Luke. Jack thought it was awfully rude of him to interrupt.

"Good. I was there when she found out. It was so hard to keep it a secret. Congratulations."

"Thanks. Sorry for cutting you off. You know…"

Luke trailed off and Jack felt the heavy shadow of two pairs of eyes staring at him. What didn't they want him to know? Was Luke promoted? To what? He was already the leader of the Hunters. Also, Gianna would not be the one to tell him. It had to be something else.

"I convinced Roy to go visit Vanessa. It took a while, but I finally got through to him."

"Good, that's good," said Luke. "You ready to go home?"

"Actually, I'll just freshen up. I'm sticking around for a go in the interview room."

"If you say so. I'll see you then."

"Bye, Luke." Jack listened to the steady taps of her boots slowly vanish into silence. Everything was quiet for a minute. He wondered if he should truly go to sleep if things were going to be this dull.

"Wow, kid. You really suck at pretending you're asleep," said Luke. Jack gritted his teeth, but otherwise did not move. "You're way too tense, you're breathing too fast…I could go on."

"Don't," he finally groaned, rolling around to see Luke. He had left the door to the holding cells open, perhaps for light. It illuminated him from behind, and Jack noticed that Luke had donned his police uniform instead of his casual clothes. He knew that it was mainly for ceremonial use or for the press, so he was most likely trying to look good in the spotlight. "I'm getting sick of your voice."

Luke scoffed and dragged a metal chair into view. He sat down, and the light from the ceiling lamps landed on an open folder in his lap. Jack watched him read in silence. He lay back on the cot and looked to see if the ceiling had anything interesting to say. Eventually, he returned to Luke.

"Whatcha doin'?"

"Reading your file."

"Anything cool?"

"No."

Silence. "How's Gianna?"

"Go back to sleep."

"I'm not tired. What was it that she told you when you went home, anyway?"

"I could get you something to eat if you want."

"I'm not hungry. If you don't tell me what she told you, I'll have to make something up..." said Jack in a sing-song voice.

"Knock yourself out."

"Is she pregnant?"

The tiny pause before Luke's stiff "no" was his answer, and not the spoken word. The silhouette's shoulders hunched around him, forming the shape of a big gloomy rock in the darkness.

"She is?" Jack grinned, happy to be right.

"I just told you no."

"Yeah, I heard. Is she keeping the baby?"

"Look, would you just shut the hell up, already?"

"No, I'm on a roll. It's yours, right? It would really suck if it wasn't."

"I am seriously thinking of coming in there and punching your face off, kid," said Luke through clenched teeth.

"That wouldn't be very nice," grumbled Jack. He fell back onto the cot and put his hands under his head. Neither of them spoke for a long time. He stared at the uneventful ceiling, wondering why Luke and Captain Stanley Roy did not try harder to find Eva and the others. His first interrogation had been about his past, perhaps to soften him up for the next round, when Roy finally asked him about his daughter. Jack had been in prison for sixteen hours. Where were his friends?

"Jack?"

"Yeah?"

Luke stared at something in the folder he held. "Was there another one of you? Another Dusk Walker, before you were wanted by the NYPD?"

"Yeah." Jack swallowed hard. Kishan had not crossed his mind in weeks, he realized guiltily.

"Well, he's mentioned briefly here. Once. Not even named." Luke tapped the folder. "But I've read this thing at least five times since we started looking for you, and I never noticed until now."

It made no sense to Jack that Kishan would even be talked about at all. He had always assumed that once the authorities had found his body, they would have categorized him as yet another victim of radiation poisoning. Although now that he thought about it...if the coroner had deduced that Kishan's date of death was later than most victims and had closely examined the body, a difference may have been noticeable.

"Can you tell me about him?" said Luke when Jack did not speak.

"Why?"

"Because I'm bored. There's still another ten minutes until your next interview."

"Until my next interrogation, you mean." Jack almost rolled onto his stomach, then was met with the sudden stench of urine. He was not to blame, since he had smelled it as soon as he entered the cell. Now he believed its origin to be the pillow. He wrinkled his nose and sat up, swinging his legs over the side of the cot. "It's not an interview room; it's an interrogation room. Why do you try to pretend otherwise?"

"The word 'interrogation' sounds a bit too harsh to

some people."

"And 'interview' isn't honest. I've seen a few movies. It can get pretty aggressive in those rooms, depending on the cop."

"Real life isn't like in the movies," said Luke. "Now tell me more about the sixth Dusk Walker."

Jack put his elbows on his thighs and looked at his hands. He was not keen to speak of Kishan to the Hunter for sentimental reasons. He missed the little Indian boy. Jack refused to allow himself to appear weak in front of Luke. He changed the subject. "How's Roy's daughter? Who attacked her?"

Luke gave a short irritated huff. "Turns out that it probably wasn't the Dusk Walkers who hurt her. Her wallet and phone were stolen. No evidence points to your friends, so we can assume that other people mugged her."

Jack smiled. He had always been certain that his friends were innocent. Knowing her, Eva would have a better strategy planned. Revenge was not her style. She preferred to get the job done cleanly—in this case, by freeing him.

"Kid, I'm serious. I want to know about your other friend."

"Fine, whatever. His name was Kishan. He was between Alix's and Lily's ages, I suppose. He had this thing where, for example, one of us would start talking about desserts, and I would say something about how good pie is. Then Kishan would start naming as many digits of pi as he could, as fast as he could."

"That was his power?" Luke did not sound convinced.

"Is it normal for a nine-year-old to name the first fifty digits of pi in less than a minute?"

"Mmm, not so much. Anything else?"

"Well, one time he named the capitals of half the countries in Africa. And not the big countries like Egypt and Algeria. I mean the tiny ones that no one can remember. Also, he could name all the presidents of the United States in order, he could do these super complicated mathematical equations aloud and stuff like that…" He stopped talking and sat up. "Wait, why do you care? A few minutes ago you were telling me to shut up. Why do you want to know about this kid who died nearly three years ago? And don't say because you're bored."

There was a short pause, and Luke ducked his head to look distractedly at the folder once more before answering. "If you tell me how he died, I'll tell you why I care. Deal?"

"Deal." He considered what he would say. For the short time Jack had known Kishan, the two of them had been inseparable. Since his death, Jack had grown used to living with four girls. Nonetheless, he wished that he could talk to someone without holding himself back as he did with Cordy, Eva, Lily, and Alix. If Kishan were still alive, that would not be a problem. Although he now considered Cordy his best friend, she was a girl, and he could not consult with her about some things that he preferred to hide from the opposite sex.

Then he realized with a pang that none of it mattered anymore. He was not simply hanging out with Luke. He was in a holding cell. Afterward, he would surely be sent to a strange lab where he would be experimented on until the end of his days. The only way that he would be able to see his friends again would be to condemn them to the same unknown, but certainly miserable fate that awaited all of them.

That was what Roy wanted. His plan all along had been for Jack to know what he had just realized on his own. The decision was impossible. His temper flared, and his nails bit into his palm. Jack thought he hated the Hunters. He was wrong. He truly despised their captain, the real brains of the team. Roy would force him to choose between his friends and his own sanity. He could not live without both. Jack immediately sat more rigidly at the idea, but Luke did not seem to notice.

"Well? You gonna talk?"

Jack swallowed hard. Perhaps talking about Kishan would even make him feel better. He had never thought that a situation like that would happen. "A month after the Explosion, Kish got sick, then he died. We assumed it was because of radiation poisoning. Happy?"

"Can't say I am, but I got the info I wanted." Luke gave a shrug. "I guess it's my turn to talk now, isn't it?"

"Yeah."

Luke cleared his throat. "This may surprise you, but I

don't know a whole lot about the Dusk Walkers. I'm not the one who's supposed to figure out every single detail about you guys in order to figure out what your next move will be. That's someone else's job."

"They've done a pretty bang-up job of that."

"Until now," corrected Luke before continuing. "Anyway, that's not my job. All I do is go where they tell me to. I just want to know more than what's on these papers. And yes, I'm also bored."

"I've got the impression that they, whoever 'they' are, don't tell you much."

"No, they don't." Luke chuckled quietly. "Also, there's another thing that's been nagging at me for a while. I don't want to give you any ideas, but…why didn't you guys just leave the city? Why stay in the place where people are looking for you?"

"Well, it's a big city. Gang activity is really common here, and we fit right in. This place just feels like home. So we stay. Other cities are too crowded, and then there's nothing to do in the suburbs. We fit in here. As long as we keep moving around, we won't get caught."

Luke gave him an amused look, staring pointedly at the vertical metal bars that separated them.

"Well, you get the idea…"

The entrance to the holding cells slid open noisily, and three figures walked in. The first had spiky blond hair that looked painful to touch. "Warren, Captain Roy wants you to—"

"To stay out," said Luke. "Don't worry, Officer, I'm leaving." He hurried up the stairs and out of Jack's sight, bringing the folder with him.

There was a rattling of keys when the second, taller officer opened the cell. Apparently the three grown men thought it required all of them to handcuff Jack before leading him out of the holding cell. Once again, the inmates in the other units jeered at him as he walked by, although this time they were not so loud.

In the interrogation room, he considered trying a different tactic when Roy or Rae would enter: He would try his best not to say a single word. It would be an understatement to say that the idea alone was a challenge in and of itself. It did not matter. He had to get out of this place as soon as possible, which meant he needed to give Cordy, Eva, Lily, and Alix more time to bust him out. Frankly, he had no idea how they could pull it off, because security inside the precinct must have at least doubled since he was arrested.

For several minutes, Jack waited, his eyelids heavy. He knew that people watched him on the other side of the one way mirror, so he stayed awake. The door opened, and he sat bolt upright, his senses back on full alert now that he had something on which to concentrate. It was Rae Anderson who sat across from Jack.

"Sorry about the wait. Had stuff to do." She reached back and smoothed her long, straight ponytail over her left shoulder.

He did not say a word. There was enough light to study her face, which was perfectly clear of any emotion. She acted like a real trained police officer, which was a refreshing change from Luke. But he was not meant to read her expression. That was what she was supposed to do to him. He could almost feel her hazel eyes on him as she watched and processed every time he swallowed, blinked, or breathed.

"So..." Rae pursed her full lips. She wore recently applied lipstick. "Do you have anything you want to tell me right now?"

Jack shook his head.

"Where are the other Dusk Walkers?"

A shrug. It was true, he thought. He did not know for sure where they were. They could still be hidden in the subway tunnels, which was unlikely. It was a habit of theirs to change their locations whenever their hideout came even close to being compromised. Perhaps they were staying at their next scheduled site. He could not be sure.

"You don't know," said Rae, putting his shrug into words. He returned her stare and noticed that her eyelashes were impossibly long. Almost every feature of her face had an artificial look, but it was just ordinary enough to be her own. She was very beautiful, but far from his type.

The first definition of beautiful that came to his mind was Eva's face. She never wore makeup, and he thought she was perfect anyway. If she could ever read his thoughts, he would probably be dead after she beat him to a pulp for thinking so. At that idea, the corners of his lips turned up a little.

"What?" said Rae.

He stopped smiling. "Nothing."

"Really?" A penciled eyebrow raised suspiciously. "So let's recap: You have no idea where the Dusk Walkers are, correct?"

He nodded.

Rae slouched a little in an impatient sigh. "All right then." She stood and walked toward the door. "You're going to stay right here. You don't get to eat, sleep, or leave this room at all until you tell us where Cordelia Lear, Eva Edwards, Lily Carlton, and Alixandra Bell are."

He hid his displeasure when he spoke. "Who came up with that plan?"

"I did." she smiled wryly.

Jack scowled. At least the interrogation room was more comfortable than the cells, and the former did not stink of urine. "I thought you were the good cop."

"You should stop thinking, Jack. It's unflattering."

CHAPTER ELEVEN

Luke typed the final words of his report, avoiding the mention of what exactly had happened in the ambulance. Roy had instructed him to keep it secret. They would have a great deal to bury if word got out about what they had done to Jack, and it could seriously damage the Hunters' credibility. Luke hoped they would never have to put the device to use, since its employment would have to be caused by, in his eyes, a disaster.

The sun was low in the sky, faded by the omnipresent clouds of the city. It cast an unsettling shadow on the part of the city that he could see out of the window. He leaned forward in his chair, his elbows on the desk. Twirling a length of his black hair between his fingers, he watched the computer screen without seeing. He thought he would have been happy after Jack was caught.

Ever since Gianna had found Luke's amnesiac self after the Explosion, his only purpose had been to find the Dusk Walkers. Now that he had accomplished part of that, he already felt that his mission was ending. Maybe he would meet the fate that Jack had predicted for him. Maybe he would find another job. He snickered at the idea. Jack was right. Luke was only a puppet, at best a circus freak. He was not meant for a real life.

His cell phone vibrated on his desk, and he picked it up to look at the small screen. He had received a text from Marial Grace. It read, 'Bottom of your drawer. Read it, shred it, then delete it.'

He wondered how she had managed to get anything into his locked desk, then decided that it would be better not to ask. Placing the phone in his pocket, Luke pulled the drawer open and rummaged through the mess inside before he found a strange document. He laid it on top of his other papers and flipped it open. The records of the five Dusk Walkers and the three Hunters were all inside. He frowned, heart sinking in disappointment. He had already seen these multiple times.

On his page, something was circled in red permanent marker. He sat up straight now, on full alert. M-G had made sure to point out his blood type: AB negative. He recalled her theory that the reason why only eight people were affected had something to do with their rare blood, which all three Hunters possessed. Since records of many New York citizens had been lost after the Explosion, they could not confirm that the Dusk Walkers were the same. Even without the latter, Luke had argued that more than eight people in the city were of the same blood type. Marial Grace was aware of the statistics, and she hypothesized that there was a second reason.

Excitement buzzed through his head. He remembered the blood sample that the doctor had taken from Jack. M-G could have seen the results before they were even sent back to the police. Luke quickly flipped to Jack's pages and understood why the folder was important. A new page was inside. Jack's blood type had been determined.

It was AB negative, just like the three Hunters.

Luke stared at the paper for a long time. What was the other factor that isolated the eight of them from all the other New Yorkers with the same blood? It was not ethnicity, nor family, nor even eye color. It had to be something that Luke could not think of. Even scientists were still stumped. After years of searching for an answer that was seemingly nonexistent, there was nothing to be found. One theory stated that since almost all other New Yorkers with the same blood time had died after the Explosion, the youth of the eight affected had made them strong enough to survive the blast. Perhaps it was mere coincidence that had brought them all together. They might never know.

Feeling that the time to destroy the files was near, he stood and walked to the paper shredder, past occupied and unoccupied desks. Since no one stood within a yard of him at the back of the room, he deemed it safe to put the pages into the shredder.

He watched the thick slices of the files fall into the basket underneath, the words tearing into pieces. When it was finally over, he picked up the plastic basket that enclosed the shreds and dumped its contents into the trash can. "Warren."

Luke looked up to find Captain Roy standing at his side. He immediately forgot about the blood types, and his attention returned to the current situation. "Did Jack say anything?"

Roy shook his head. "Nope. He knows everything, but he won't talk." His eyes were bloodshot. The captain never even looked sad, let alone shed a tear. Luke did not press on. Vanessa had to be in awful condition.

"Well, I've got nothing," said Luke. His eyes fell on the clock on the wall. "It's late. Is there any chance that the Dusk Walkers will be out tonight?"

"Doubt it," said Roy. "They may be young, but they've had a decent strategy. Now that everyone's on the lookout for them because of last night, they won't come out for at least a week. They snatched enough food from the grocery store to hold them for that long."

"Right. So our only chance of finding the other Dusk Walkers before they cause anymore damage is—"

"Is for Turner to tell us where they are. Exactly."

"Crap."

"By now, he's figured out that if we have all five of them in custody, they won't just be locked away in a jail cell. I've taken a look around that test lab, and I've got to tell you…it ain't no children's hospital."

Luke cringed at the images that appeared in his head when picturing the lab, mostly inspired by horror and science fiction movies. "Sir, last week you said that I'd get to take a look around the lab. Any updates about that?"

Roy shook his head. "I haven't yet agreed on a date with them. I'm sure you'll get to see the place soon."

Luke could only think of what Jack had told him earlier. He dreaded that secrets were being kept from him.

Maybe instead of being killed, they would be sent to rot in a test lab with the Dusk Walkers. It sounded even worse than dying. From now on, Luke promised himself that he would watch his back. Especially around Roy, no matter how difficult it would be.

Luke now noticed every detail of his captain's expression: the thick brows that sunk low over his eyes, the skin that wrinkled on his dark bald head, the corners of the moustache that curled up slightly. Luke had grown greatly suspicious in the matter of a few hours. He would leave nothing to chance.

"What if they try to bust him out?"

"Repeat that using proper nouns."

"The Dusk Walkers. What if they come to rescue Jack? How's our security?"

"Tight," Roy assured him. "There's no way a bunch of kids can get past the patrols and alarms that we have, with or without superpowers."

There was no warning before the room went entirely black. Luke heard no faint whoosh that would indicate a loss of power. He squinted and saw nothing, not even when he waved his hand in front of his eyes. The light that the setting sun would have provided was not enough to aid his sight. It was too dark for a Hunter.

"Hey, who turned out the lights?" said a moron across the room in a stage whisper.

"Do you see anything?" said Luke to Roy.

"No, it's pitch black." If even Roy was blind, something was wrong. There should have been just enough daylight for normal people to see only a little.

Luke's cell phone chimed in his pocket, and he withdrew it, hoping for answers. As he looked down at where the screen should have lit up, he saw nothing, but it still rang. "Hello?"

"Luke?"

"Rae! What's going on?"

"I have no idea...so the lights are out where you are too, I'm guessing?"

"Yeah, it's got to be the Dusk Walkers."

"Maybe," said Rae. "Can you explain how everything still works, yet we can't see a single thing?"

Luke thought for a moment, not finding a single logical way that the kids could cause everyone to go blind at the same time. "No, but is that our priority right now? You're in the observation room, right? Can you see if Jack's still in there?"

"I've got no clue, Luke. I can't even find the door right now."

"Then find it! I've been working too hard to get this far. We can't let him get away." When he raised his voice, he heard nearly everyone in the room go quiet. He was grateful they could not see his face go red.

"Don't talk to me like that! I've been working just as hard as you this year, and you get all the credit! How is that fair?"

Luke was about to tell her something about the fairness of life, but Roy cut him off. "Give me the phone."

He almost protested, but after deciding that it would not get him very far, he held the phone toward Roy's general direction. Moments later, the captain was talking to Rae. He lowered his voice as people resumed talking.

"Anderson, listen up. Both of you are tired and stressed. I get that. But if you took a breath and thought about this a little, you would remember why you took Turner into the ambulance and not into a NYPD vehicle."

Luke's mouth hung open in astonishment as he realized Roy's plan. "You're going to let him go? Gianna said that she wasn't sure if her bug would work long-distance or not, and we can't risk that!"

"Well, we're going to have to."

He ran his fingers through his hair. "This is insane."

"Last time I checked, I'm your captain, and I call the shots. Not you." The next sentences were for Rae. "We'll call you back in ten minutes if the lights aren't back on by then. And whatever you do, don't go into the interview room."

☢

Jack tapped the table with the tips of his fingers to the beat of a popular rock song. His eyesight slid in and out of focus as he struggled to stay awake. He was nearly tempted to tell Rae where the Dusk Walkers were just so that he could sleep.

The room went black. He sat upright, thinking for a moment that he had dozed off. But the darkness was real. Maybe everyone had forgotten about him and had gone home, or they wanted to save energy by turning out the lights. Jack doubted both possibilities, so he jumped to the next option: The Dusk Walkers were coming for him. The thought alone made him want to jump up and down in glee.

He stayed very quiet, waiting for the door to open. Then finally, among all of the commotion of confused cops outside, there was a barely audible creaking of the door, and two pairs of footsteps approached. He stood, handcuffs still biting into his wrists.

Jack opened his mouth to speak, but an unfamiliar girl's voice stopped him.

Try not to make any noise. No one can know we're here or we're dead.

The voice had not spoken aloud. It was in his head. At first he thought that his mind had spoken to him, although he did not see why his mind would speak in a girl's voice. Then he had the strange feeling that the speaker was one of the people in the room. "Who—"

Shut up! Bloody knickers, what don't you get about 'don't make any noise'?

The use of the expression stumped him for a moment, since the voice sounded very much American. When he shook it off, he almost asked again who they were, then the girl continued to speak.

We're going to get you out of here. Just follow my brother and we'll talk later.

He would much rather talk now, but she had a point. Even though the cops in the building were spinning in confused circles, that did not mean that the next few minutes would be easy. Would they have to follow the walls to get out, or could the two siblings see in the unexplained dark? Apparently, the brother knew where he was going, because he grabbed Jack's forearm with calloused fingers and guided him confidently out of the interview room. He heard the girl close behind him and the cacophony of the bewildered police officers around them. When they turned a corner, Jack's shoulder slammed into someone who seemed to be walking the opposite way.

"Jesus!" said an unknown baritone voice. "Sorry, can't see a thing."

Before Jack could answer, the boy pulled his arm roughly, and they continued their hurried walk. A door opened, blowing a draft of cool, polluted air into his face. They were outside. However, when Jack looked around, something was wrong. He still saw nothing. He was certain that the sun had not completely set. Even if it had, the moon and streetlamps would have lit their way.

Yes, we're outside. Keep walking, and we'll stop once we're away from here.

Judging by the horrible stench, they ended up behind a busy restaurant just before garbage day. Jack coughed and wrinkled his nose. Then the lights came back on.

He blinked repeatedly to get used to the change in brightness. The glow of the streetlamps illuminated the trio as he stared at his rescuers. Two figures a few inches shorter than him pulled off patterned ski masks and cotton mittens to reveal a couple of freckly teenagers. They both had the same wavy brown hair, the girl's longer than the boy's, and electric blue eyes that almost glowed in the dark. Matching button noses and dimpled smiles were identical to both of their faces. He concluded that they were twins, no older than fifteen.

Jack narrowed his eyes. "Are you two insane?"

"No, we've been tested." The girl grinned toothily.

He arched his eyebrows. So they were insane. They must have recently escaped from a mental hospital, although their sophisticated clothing indicated otherwise. The girl wore a long beige trench coat. Underneath were navy-blue leggings and black leather boots, and a matching scarf was around her neck. The boy, on the other hand, wore a dark button-down shirt. His beige slacks matched his sister's jacket, almost as though they wanted to be identical. These two were no street rats.

"Right. So who the hell are you, what just happened with the lights, and why are you helping me?" he said before either of them could speak again.

"I'm Meg," said the girl. "I can read minds, and I can also speak to people in their heads, like I did with you earlier."

Jack did not really have a choice but to believe what she said. After all, she had spoken to him already. He could not hide his glee. Other people had powers, people who did not want to kill him.

"This is my brother William. He's three whole minutes younger than me," she continued, pointing at the surly boy. "He can—"

"Control light particles," finished William. "Back in the precinct, I basically bent the particles to surround us with darkness. I can see through it, but it's still fuzzy. Like night vision, sort of."

"Now for your final question: Why are we helping you?" said Meg. "Easy. We're like you. We saw on the telly that you'd been caught, and the only thing that we could do was rescue you."

"Were you in the Explosion three years ago?" Jack saw that they still had suntans from the recent summer, so they were unlike the Dusk Walkers, who could not stand natural light. However, they seemed to manage well in the low glow of the street, unlike the Hunters.

"No. Our dad is the head of a big company, and when Mum got pregnant, she volunteered for this huge experiment to look good for the press. She died in childbirth, and we came out like this."

"Wait, you've been like this your entire lives?" He had thought it difficult to have powers for three years. He could not imagine having them since he was born and remembering the whole experience.

"Yeah," said William. "It's tough sometimes because no one can know, but we deal with it. We keep out of trouble for the most part, and that's worked for a long time now."

"Does your dad know what you are?"

"Well, he knows that I'm a whiz in all of my subjects at school and that I'm a musician." William smiled proudly. "But no, he doesn't know that we have powers. No one does."

"Anyway, I prefer to think of being like this as more of a 'who' than a 'what,'" said Meg. "We're still human. That's what people don't understand. They don't understand that the reason why you and the other Dusk Walkers break into stores for food is because they rejected you. It isn't the other way around. I think I'm right by saying that sometimes, you're not so sure either."

"Are you reading my mind?" said Jack.

"I didn't need to read your mind for that."

"Yeah, whatever." A scoff escaped his lips. He turned on his heels and began to walk across the street.

"Where are you going?"

"Away from you two! You're freaking me out. You…you talk too much."

"We're in District One, Jack," said William. "It's a

pretty long walk to get all the way back to the Dusk Walkers. Wouldn't they be in District Three?"

"We can drive you back," said Meg. "We don't have our licenses yet, but as long as we don't pass the speed limit, we'll be all right."

Jack stopped in the middle of the empty street, hearing the commotion that rose from the direction of the police department. He needed to escape quickly. The twins had gone through the trouble of busting him out of jail, so he could trust them. Even if they were crazy, they were his only hope of getting back to his friends.

He finally gave in and followed the twins into a parking garage. William climbed into the driver's seat of an old Toyota Camry, Meg slid into the back, and Jack got into the passenger seat. "I thought you said that you don't have a license," said Jack as William withdrew a ring of keys.

"We don't. This is our dad's. We nicked it so we could come get you."

"You do realize that if a cop stops us, I'm dead, and both of you are dead too, just for being seen with me." He looked at William. "So drive carefully."

CHAPTER TWELVE

"Home, sweet home."

District Three was empty. The poorest parts of town were located there, and everyone else kept well enough away. The more recently abandoned homes still had running water, which attracted the Dusk Walkers to the area.

Jack instructed William to stop in front of a tiny bungalow that was situated deep into the District, close to the water. The twins followed him up the loosely paved sidewalk, where the bricks shifted under his feet, and he stumbled in his hurry. He finally arrived at the peeling green door and knocked three times.

"Wait here. I'll be right back," he said to the twins before jogging to the other side of the house. Their secret knock consisted of tapping three times on the front door, and if the person knocked again on the back door, then it was safe to assume that the stranger was in fact a Dusk Walker.

He rapped on the second door and waited, his heart racing. He had been away from his friends for an entire day. That had never happened before. He shifted his weight from foot to foot, ready to walk in by himself, which would only guarantee that he would be the target of a 'maim first, ask questions later' attack. So he waited, glancing at the windows of the house. All of them were boarded shut to block out the light for when the sun was in the sky. That indicated that they had at least been there.

He knocked again in case they hadn't heard him before. The door opened slowly. Cordy's wide, brown eyes were the first things he saw, and they stared at him in disbelief.

"Holy..." Her fingers lifted to touch her parted lips. He grinned uncontrollably at the sight of her until his cheeks ached. "We were so worried about you. Are you okay? No one followed you?"

Jack stepped into the house and hugged her with one arm. "I'm fine, Dee. No one followed me. Well, not any cops, at least—"

He froze. The three other Dusk Walkers had come into view. Cordy slipped discreetly out from under his arm just in time for someone else to throw their own arms around his neck. He was nearly sent to the ground, but he threw his foot back and closed the door with his heel to keep himself upright. He closed his eyes, the faded scent of strawberry shampoo filling his senses, and he hugged Eva back tightly, forgetting that anyone else was in the room.

Jack came crashing back to reality when someone cleared her throat. Upon opening his eyes, he saw that Lily laughed silently at him. He smiled and winked in return. Eva took a step back.

"Hi," she said. "I shouldn't have left you at the garage, I'm sorry."

"Hey, it wasn't your fault. You did the right thing." She nodded and returned her hands to the pockets of her sweater. "Oh."

"What?"

"Well, in my version of the past few seconds, you said something cheesy like 'I thought that I'd never see you again,' then you kissed me."

Eva stared back, her fair brows knitted together, and he felt his cheeks flush. "I'd rather kiss a frog."

"What about a frog prince?"

"As long as it isn't you." When she smirked playfully, Jack was free to assume that she was kidding. He picked up Alix, who had been waiting with her arms open.

"Jesus, Al! You're gonna have to skip a few meals if you want me to keep doing this."

She giggled and clung to his neck as though he was her only lifeline. He tugged on one of her braids with his free hand. It was tempting to go to the next room and collapse onto the old couch, then he remembered that the twins still waited outside.

"I've got something to show you guys. I wouldn't believe you if you told me that you thought I busted out of prison all by myself." He put the heavy youngster back on the ground, much to her displeasure. Then he took her hand to make up for it, turning to lead them all to the front door. He opened it to find Meg and William sitting on the front steps.

"Who're they?" said Lily.

The twins stood in unison and began to explain everything, exactly how Jack had heard it in the alley. This time, William managed to speak louder than his sister. From what he already knew about the siblings, this was quite an accomplishment.

☢

Jack took a quick shower to wash off all the dirt and grime he was covered in, then pulled on fresh clothes. The girls had faithfully brought back his bag from the parking garage, which meant that all of his possessions were returned to him at last.

He toweled his wet hair, then stepped out of the bathroom to find Eva and Meg talking on the couch in low voices. "Yo."

"Hiya."

"Why are you still here?" he asked Meg while he pulled out and unwrapped an energy bar that sat at the bottom of his backpack.

"Gosh," she mumbled. "You'd think that after saving this wanker's arse, I'd have earned some respect."

"I didn't mean it like that! Won't your dad wonder where you are? It's getting late." He bit into the chocolate snack. After not eating all day, it was like paradise to his taste buds.

"He's on a business trip and won't be back until Saturday."

"What business?"

"Communications."

Jack nodded, incapable of answering with his mouth full. When he swallowed, he held up his old shirt and jacket. After his brief time in prison, he did not want to wear the same clothes again. The Dusk Walkers did not care for dry cleaning, only stealing new outfits when they saw fit. "I'm just going to toss these in a dumpster. I shouldn't be long; it's only a block away."

"Be careful," said Eva when he walked past her.

"Yep!" he said through another mouthful of energy bar.

When he stepped outside, the chilly night air welcomed him in his thin T-shirt. Goose bumps rose on his bare arms, but he liked the cold. It kept him alert, but not acutely so. While the lights from District One glowed in the distant sky, the street he stood on was deserted. For a moment he felt desperately alone, then he remembered that he was back with his friends. His many hours spent in custody were a memory now. At that thought, a smile spread on his face, and he continued toward his destination.

The dumpster behind the vacant café was nearly empty. When he peered inside, there were only a few skeletal rats and a take-out paper bag that looked at least a month old. He threw his wrapper and ruined clothes into the massive metal box, and the revolting smell of aging rats and month-old hamburgers wafted into the air. He gagged, almost regretting the energy bar that he had just devoured.

Resisting the urge to vomit, he stumbled away from the dumpster, only to feel the barrel of a gun against the back of his head. "Having a good night?" said the voice he dreaded the most.

He froze, and his stomach performed a back flip. If Luke had found him, there was a good chance that he knew where the others were too. By returning to them, Jack had walked directly into a trap. His love for his friends had gotten the best of him. How could he have been so stupid? He hadn't even considered the consequences of his actions, as usual. On the other hand, he could only wonder how Luke had found him so quickly. The darkness that William had created in the precinct should have slowed down the Hunters.

"How'd you know I was here?"

"I suppose it doesn't really matter if I tell you now…" Luke put his hand on Jack's shoulder and turned him around. "You're bugged!"

"What?"

"You heard me."

"But…" His mind reeled, wondering when Luke could have possibly had the time to put any sort of tracking device on him without noticing. He mentally retraced his steps of the past day. Then he remembered. "The ambulance?"

"We didn't drug you for nothing, you know."

"I don't believe this." Jack combed his hair back with his fingers. That was what he and Rae had done to him while he had been unconscious. Now all he had to do was figure out where it was hidden…

"Well, you're going to have to believe it." Luke lifted his pistol and pointed it between Jack's eyes. "Now, last words?"

"Huh?"

The Hunter frowned. "I'm going to assume you didn't hear what I said, because that's a pretty awful last word."

"Whoa, whoa, wait a second…you're going to kill me?"

"That's the general idea when someone asks for your last words, isn't it?"

"Why? Wh…what happened to the labs and the high-security prisons and all that?" Jack waved his hands around to express his point, but he probably just looked stupid.

"Change of plans," said Luke. "Roy's decided that we've spent too long hunting you down only for you to escape the next day. He told me to just put an end to it so that it doesn't happen again. It would be so much cheaper and easier for us if you were out of the way."

Jack's skin crawled up his arms, leaving his fingers numb. He gave a quick shiver. Dead, he would be out of the way, as though he were an object. And what had he contributed to the world? Fear and lies. Once he would be gone, he would be nothing. He swallowed hard. "Will you do the same to the others?"

It took a moment for Luke to answer. When he ultimately did, his voice was strained, regretful. "Yes. I'm not so jazzed about that part, but it's got to be done."

"No, it doesn't," said Jack. He could cope with dying. He was not worth much. But he could not imagine Eva's dead body, or Cordy's, or Lily's, or Alix's. He would take a bullet for them any day, as long as it was worth it.

"You've got two options, kid. You've always had two options: Either you come quietly, or we take you away in body bags. You've always refused the first, and even taking you in by force didn't work. This is what it has to come to." Luke's voice grew quieter, which Jack prayed meant he was reluctant to kill.

"Well…how do you even know that I'll die? I can heal, right? What if I can come back to life after I die?" Jack was stalling now. He didn't know what else to do.

"I don't think you want to take that chance."

"The Wolverine can come back to life after he dies!" Jack slowly lowered his hand and reached behind him, feeling the handle of the knife that was in his belt.

"The Wolverine's a fictional character."

"Yeah, well...whatever." He stared at the gun between his eyes, imagining the bullet shooting out and lodging itself in his brain. The verdict? It would be uncomfortable.

"Look, kid, I'm sorry about this. I really am," said Luke, his finger on the trigger. He was really going to shoot, and Jack had run out of things to say. That had never happened before. "If I had the choice, I wouldn't do it—ARGH!"

Jack swiftly brought his blade down, tearing a deep, three-inch gash in Luke's right forearm. He did not look back. His heart pumped adrenaline-crammed blood through his whole body as he ran, and his feet pounded against the pavement faster than he could keep track. He had almost reached the main road when he heard the gun fire.

He collapsed, crashing to the cold, rough asphalt before he even knew what had happened. "Nngh," he grunted, his eyelids fluttering as he recovered. Air struggled to return to his lungs, but apart from that he was not hurt. It took him longer than it should have to realize that a warm body lay on top of his—Eva's. His heart had been racing before, though now it felt as though it beat so fast that it had died.

"You all right?" Their noses almost touched. For the first time in three years, he noticed that the forest green of her irises grew darker closer to her pupils. It looked like an endless tunnel to somewhere unknown and, hopefully, nice. Then he remembered that she had spoken. He would try to answer with something cool and smart, perhaps something that suggested her help annoyed him.

"Um...I...uh huh. I'm okay."

Eva raised a pale eyebrow, then raised her head. Luke stood above them, holding his gun with both of his hands. His sleeve was drenched in crimson blood, and his right hand held the pistol more loosely than the other. When Jack tried to slide out from under Eva, Luke pointed the gun at him, his left finger resting on the trigger.

"Don't get up."

They remained sitting.

"I thought you were supposed to be fast. Why couldn't you dodge the knife?" Jack nodded at their opponent's wounded arm. Seeing how much it bled, he could not help but feel a great sense of pride, since his knife had rarely come in handy.

"I can't see the future, and I can't slow down time," said Luke bluntly. "I didn't see that coming, so I couldn't get out of the way fast enough. Now stop talking. I'm supposed to shoot you."

Jack gulped audibly. He had been in trouble before, but this time it seemed as though he was not going to escape. The tip of Eva's finger brushed his hand. He looked at her, and she gave him the smallest nod that he had ever seen. It meant something, but he did not know quite what it would be. Maybe she just wanted to hold his hand, since they were about to die. Despite the peculiarity of the thought, he quite liked that idea.

He understood. She intended to use her ninja-like abilities to fight Luke off. He shook his head a fraction to the side. She was agile, but the Hunter was fast. Superhumanly fast. She would not be able to beat him.

Someone cleared her throat. It was not Jack, nor Eva, nor Luke. Jack whirled around, and he smiled when he saw Meg, William, and the three other Dusk Walkers. In front of them marched Rae, her hands raised at shoulder height in surrender.

"Rae?"

"Luke?" She stared at Luke's arm, sounding just as concerned as him.

"It's just a flesh wound." He stared at Meg and William. "Who're they?"

Rae shrugged.

"Here's the deal, you sods: We'll let her go if you let Jack and Eva walk safely back this way," said Meg. Her words were well-rehearsed, but Jack heard her insecurity at the sight of the gun. "If not...she gets turned into puppy food."

"Yum." Lily chuckled. In the light of the streetlamps, Jack saw that her mouth and nose had morphed into a dog's muzzle. He and Eva laughed, despite the circumstances.

It took a shockingly short time for Luke to decide to holster his gun and to step away.

"All right, Rae. We're outnumbered. Let's go." He nodded at Jack, which the latter took as permission for him and Eva to stand. Jack kept his eyes locked on his enemy as they walked away slowly. He did not underestimate Luke, who could easily pull his gun back out and shoot him in the back. There was something that did not feel right.

Luke mouthed a single word: "Bugged."

CHAPTER THIRTEEN

Jack halted in his tracks. That was why Luke had let him go. That was why he had let himself monologue earlier. No matter where Jack would hide, no matter how many times he would escape, the Hunters would always be able to find him. There was only one solution. It was the only way that he could keep the others safe.

Eva pulled his arm, and they safely arrived next to Meg, William, and the Dusk Walkers. Luke and Rae turned their backs and walked down the main road until they disappeared.

"That was awful," said Meg.

"That was nothing," said Jack. William glared at him, although the look was hardly harmful. The other boy was as pale as a sheet.

"They left really quickly; it was weird." Cordy shivered. "What did they want?"

"As long as they're gone, I don't care how fast they left or what they came for in the first place," said Lily, shaking her muzzle-less head.

"Jack?" said Eva, ignoring everyone else. She leaned

closer. "What's wrong?"

He unclenched his jaw, his mind numb. "Here's the plan: Meg and William will go home. If they've got any sense, they'll stay there. The rest of you will go to location four."

Location four was an abandoned building in what had once been Queens. It would take the better part of an hour to reach even by public transportation, but they would not attract attention there.

"And you're coming with us, right?" said Alix, seeing right through his plan. He could not lie, especially not to her. She would be heartbroken when the time came for him to leave.

He shook his head, looking to the ground to avoid their expressions. "I can't. When they caught me yesterday, they bugged me. That's how Luke and Rae were able to find us, and that's why they gave up so easily. The only way for you all to stay safe is if I'm not with you."

"What's the plan, then?" said Eva. If he didn't know better, he would claim that her voice was breaking. "You're just going to take a stroll around the city and wait for them to find you and kill you?"

Jack looked back up. He could have been imagining things, but he thought he saw tears in her eyes. "Yeah. Why, is there something wrong with that?"

"How about the part where you die? Or doesn't that matter to you?"

He stared at her without blinking. He had not intended to make her this upset. Managing a hesitant smile, he poked her shoulder. "I knew you cared about me."

"Of course I care about you." She narrowed her eyes. "We all care about you."

Yes, he knew that. He would always know that. He had never thought the opposite for one second. The Dusk Walkers loved him as much as he loved them, and nothing would ever prove the contrary. Especially not the little head that rammed into his chest. He winced and looked at Alix, whose face was buried in his T-shirt.

"I don't want you to go…" she mumbled. "You just got back."

Jack could only put his arms around her. "I'm sorry. D'you want to walk back to the house with me so I can get my things?"

When Alix stepped back, she wiped away a tear on her cheek before she nodded. Seeing her so sad, he almost wanted to change his mind and stay with them. He reminded himself that he was leaving for their own good, which only helped a little. He took her hand as they crossed the street, the others not far behind.

"No parties while I'm gone, okay? Wait at least a week." Jack turned his bag upside-down on the couch, separating the food from his personal belongings. He would have no need for grub where he intended to go.

The remaining Dusk Walkers could split it among themselves. "Don't let the neighbors know you're there, don't eat all the food at once, change houses every eight or nine days, and only steal stuff if the door is closed or has a small alarm system. Watch your backs, and if all else fails…I'll see you in heaven."

"That's not funny," said Cordy. Her chin scrunched up, as she did when she tried not to cry. He should have left straight away. He was only making it harder on himself and on his friends. Looking at their faces now, he did not want to leave.

"I'm not laughing." He pulled on a new sweater. It was a green hoodie that he had lifted from a store nearly half a year ago. He liked it so much because it reminded him of Eva's eyes, which he had never told to anybody. Taking a glance around the living room, he saw Lily, curled up on the other side of the couch. Alix sat in the armchair, fiddling with the hem of her jeans, while Cordy and Eva perched on both of the arms. Meg and William stood near the door, ready to leave when he did. The twins had given all of them their cell phone numbers in case the Dusk Walkers ever needed help.

Jack had one more thing to say before he left. "Dee, can I talk to you in private?"

Everyone's eyes followed him and Cordy to the kitchen. His fingers trembled. He gritted his teeth and noticed with a sinking feeling that he had no pockets where he could hide his hands. He leaned against the dusty counter and spotted a plastic grocery bag that looked new. Inside he found a carton of orange juice and a stack of paper cups. He unscrewed the cap and unsealed it.

"Look," he said in a low voice. He knew that at least Lily would be listening in because of her curiosity and her ability to grow ultrasensitive ears, and he did not want to make things too easy for her. His words were for Cordy. "You'll be the oldest once I'm gone. And I've seen the way you take care of Alix. I know you can be responsible."

"Are you asking me to become the leader? Didn't we decide to never have one?"

"That's not exactly what I'm asking." He poured himself the juice and lifted it to his lips, glad to have his hands busy. It would likely be the last thing that he ate or drank. It was an odd thing to consider, seeing as he had never liked orange juice very much.

"Then you're giving me the 'take care of the others while I'm dead' speech." Cordy crossed her arms over her chest. The purple turtleneck she wore was too small. Her wrist bones peeked out from the sleeve, and a slit of skin on her sharp hips was revealed. Jack stepped forward to pull down the shirt, but she pushed his hand away. She tugged on the fabric until she was properly covered, then looked back at him. "I don't get why you can't stay. I mean, we can hold our own in a fight, we've proved that a few times already. And especially with Meg and William on our side, the Hunters are both outnumbered and outpowered."

"They'll just keep coming back. We don't have the advantage of hiding in the dark anymore. The twins have to go home sometime, and honestly, we're not strong enough to beat all three Hunters at once. Eventually, they'll bring in the big guns, and we'll be screwed. It's safer if I leave."

"Yeah. Fine, whatever." Cordy scoffed and rolled her eyes. A tear rolled down her cheek. She hurriedly dried her face and turned away. Jack finished his orange juice and put the cup down. The more he lingered, the faster the Hunters would find him. He had to leave.

"Look—" Jack stiffened. There were shadows on the walls, shadows that were not theirs. Small and tall shapes alike moved around the kitchen, vanishing after a few steps. He counted at least a dozen ghosts in the room. They did not yet take form, but they still gave him goose bumps. This had happened before. In front of anyone else, the ghosts would have stayed invisible and minded their own business, but Cordy sometimes lost control and brought them forward. "Dee…"

"Go away," she sobbed, pressing the heels of her palms against her temples. Jack retreated until he understood that she was not speaking to him. "Get out!"

The ghosts faded at her command, but Cordy's cheeks remained wet. Jack walked up to her, his limbs heavy with grief. He hugged her tightly.

"I'm sorry." Her voice was muffled against him. "There are just a lot of people who died here, a long time ago."

"Shh, it's all right." He closed his eyes, stroking her black sheet of hair. The embrace was not only to comfort her about her powers, but it would be the last time he held her. A soreness in his throat kept him from saying anything else.

Jack blinked his heavy eyelids open. Eva stood in the entranceway and held out his backpack. She had kept a level head, knowing that he had to leave as soon as possible. Luke would only need to spend a few hours at the most in the hospital, then he would come after Jack.

"Bye," said Eva. He did not want to remember her as she was now. The skin around her eyes was red and swollen. He would remember her as she was only fifteen minutes ago, when she had nearly taken a bullet for him.

Jack and Cordy separated, and he took the near-empty bag. He swung it over his back and tugged his collar out from under the straps with clumsy fingers. The three of them left the kitchen with solemn steps, as though they were at a funeral. In a way, they were. The government would surely not let his body be revealed to the public. Despite his death, he would still be the subject of experiments. A chill crawled down his spine at the thought of people carving up his corpse, but it was a possibility.

Neither Alix nor Lily spoke. The younger girl hugged him, and the other only gripped his hand briefly. He did not linger to wonder if it was a handshake or a friendly touch, but it would be their last.

With his fingers on the doorknob, Jack stopped in front of the door and looked back. He let his eyes rest on each of his companions, soon to be left without him. He let their faces be absorbed into his memory, then he pulled the door open before he could decide to stay.

He stepped outside, followed by the twins, and the three of them walked in silence toward the red car.

He thought of how the four girls would manage without him. He would be their first loss since Kishan, and the group had grown much closer since then. In his absence, Cordy would be the motherly figure to the two youngest Dusk Walkers, and Eva would be the strategist, figuring out their next moves. Lily would be the joker of the bunch, morphing her face into funny animal shapes. Alix would keep them all warm with her fire and her hugs that healed all bad feelings. Frankly, not much would change. Jack did not do much aside from being the pain in the ass of the group, which he grasped with a pang.

The trio finally arrived at the twins' car.

"Well, I guess this is it," said William.

"Yeah…I'll see you on the other side, then." Jack gave a nervous smile. "Thanks for breaking me out of prison."

The twins climbed into the car. As they pulled away, Meg waved at him sadly. He returned the salute weakly and stood still until the sound of the engine disappeared. When silence fell once more, he turned on his heels and began to walk in the direction of District Two.

CHAPTER FOURTEEN

"Tell me if you're dying," said Rae.

"I will." Luke leaned against the seat of the car. Since there were no working hospitals in District Three, their destination would take longer to reach. The wound in his arm bled more than he had expected. He had to put pressure on the cut with an old shirt to stop the hemorrhage. It was only after the adrenaline rush wore off that it had started to hurt. The pain varied from dull pulses to short spikes of white-hot agony. Luke gritted his teeth and bore it. He would survive.

Rae stared blankly at the road ahead, her eyes unmoving and her lips tight. Sometimes he thought she was a robot who came from another planet because of her hard and solitary attitude. It was difficult to tell what was on her mind, or if something was wrong.

"Are we there yet?"

"Five minutes." Rae gave a sigh and pushed her golden hair behind her ear. He realized she had never asked him if he was all right. Of course he was, but it was considered polite to ask, to his knowledge. Typical Rae.

Luke wanted to rest his eyes for a moment, then his phone buzzed in his pocket. He gave a small start at the unexpected text and checked his messages. It was from Gianna: "Successful mission?"

He adjusted the shirt against his arm in a way that he could support itself, then typed an answer with his free hand. 'No—heading to hospital.'

'You okay?'

'Only a flesh wound. No big.'

'And the Dusk Walkers?'

'J knows about the bug. Can get them later.'

'Okay. Love you.'

'Love you too.'

Gianna did not answer after that, so Luke returned his phone to his pocket.

"Who was that?" said Rae.

"It was Gee. I filled her in."

She acknowledged the answer by not asking anymore questions. There was not much time to say anything in any case. They had arrived at the hospital. Rae parked the car and stepped out. Luke started to follow her, then she made a gesture for him to stop. "I'll try to get us in fast."

"No, there are people waiting there who are doing

worse than me."

"It's not that. We need to get back on the Dusk Walkers' trail. Also, I'd rather no one knew about you getting hurt, so we can't spend an hour in the ER for everyone to see."

Luke groaned in protest. "At least call the captain to see what he thinks."

She stared at him blankly for a moment, her jaw set. She thought he was an idiot for thinking of other people, but he could live with that. Then she reached into her jacket pocket, tapped a few keys on her phone, and brought it to her ear.

"Captain, it's Anderson…We didn't get the Dusk Walkers, but…Yes, exactly. Anyway, Luke was hurt, and we're in front of the hospital now. I was wondering if it would be a good idea to try to get him in first so we can get out quick and avoid any trouble. Here he is." She passed the phone to Luke.

"Captain?"

"Warren, she's right," said Roy. "In a situation like this, you get priority over most patients."

"A situation like this is a cop who needs a few stitches."

"No, it's the lead Hunter who needs to get back to his job. Get fixed up and report back as soon as you're done."

"Yes, Sir," said Luke bitterly. "There's one more thing: There were two other kids when we found the Dusk Walkers. They could be twins."

"And?"

"And they were on the Dusk Walkers' side. I think they might have powers too."

"Take them out as well."

His jaw dropped. "But—"

"I'm your captain, Warren. Do as I say." The line disconnected. Roy had hung up. Luke lowered the phone, stunned. Rae took it from him.

"What's the verdict?" she said, completely oblivious to what their captain had just asked of him.

"Try to get me in first."

"Okay. Wait here." She locked the door as she walked toward the entrance of the hospital. It had begun to rain. The wind lifted as well, blowing her hair backward when she hurried inside.

Luke did not tell her about Roy's new orders. Having to kill the Dusk Walkers was horrible enough. Now they had to put down a couple of kids whom they knew nothing about. There was something wrong with Roy, he knew it. Perhaps it had something to do with Vanessa's attack. It was the only thing that Luke knew of that could have triggered something inside the captain.

He opened the glove compartment, where there were five folders inside. Each contained the information that had been accumulated about the Dusk Walkers. The first was the most familiar to Luke, being the one that he had read several times. He placed Jack's folder under the others and picked up the next one. He felt the need to get to know the children he was about to kill.

The picture on the top was of a thirteen-year-old Cordy, wearing two braids in her hair and shiny braces on her teeth. Underneath the old photo he found a recent wanted poster of her, all of the pictures gathered from the crimes she committed, each of her childhood report cards, and a written interview with her parents. He skimmed her biography. A quiet student with a B average, Cordy's parents divorced when she was eleven. She had two older sisters named Lana and Melissa.

The next folder was about Eva Edwards, containing the same kind of documents as Cordy's. She was an only child, and her parents were both schoolteachers. According to the interview, she was at the top of all of her classes. Not only was she an excellent student, but she was involved in athletic activities nearly every evening after school.

Luke opened the fourth folder at his disposal: Lily's. The fact about her that stood out was her known love for animals. The fifth-grader had been involved in nothing but furry, scaly, and winged creatures since her first steps. Her mother was a veterinarian, and her father had grown up on a farm, which had likely incited her passion.

Alix's parents often worked overtime and left her with her teenage stepbrother. According to her teachers, she misbehaved often, but it was nothing out of the ordinary for a second-grader. Luke remembered that she was ten years old now, and he felt sick to his stomach. He would have to kill her. He asked himself what would happen if he avoided completing his mission. The Hunters would no longer have the excuse of being incapable of finding the children, so he could not use that against Roy. Because of Jack's microchip, they knew exactly where the Dusk Walkers were.

Luke recalled the inception of the Hunters and their precinct. They had spoken to each of the young criminals' families, aside from Jack's father, who had refused to present himself. Each relative had demanded the same thing: Luke's team was to be cautious with their children. Despite the chaos, each parent wanted their youngster safe and returned to them once they were found. That could not happen now. He doubted Roy would wait before sending the bodies straight to the test lab.

Luke had never spoken to his parents. They were abroad, and he did not want to bother them. He could not imagine the grief of raising a son, only to have him forget his past. Luke still remembered bits and pieces of his lost years, but they were no more than visions of a house or memories of a perfume. He knew that Gianna and Rae had contacted both of their parents before, but they had not remained close. Nevertheless, he counted them as lucky.

His phone buzzed. Rae had sent him a text: 'You're in.' The lock mechanism clicked open, and he saw that she stood near the door through which she had entered. When Luke stepped out of the car, holding his injured arm against his chest, he was able to reach her in under a second. Rae lifted her keys and pressed the button to lock the car once more.

"The doctor just has to finish fixing some kid's broken arm, then it's your turn." Rae returned her keys to her pocket.

"That was fast."

"You're a superhero. It's an honor to help you out."

Luke knew that she was sarcastic, so he did not acknowledge her comment. "Can we just get this over with?"

They went inside and were directed into a small sterile room. The doctor there was tall and spoke in an accent that Luke could not identify. She treated his wound, then quickly sewed on his stitches. It took no longer than fifteen minutes, but he had to stay in the waiting room for another ten minutes. Rae picked up a celebrity magazine to read while Luke took a quick glance at the children playing with the games at the center of the room. He would soon be the father to one like them. Goodness, what had he gotten himself into?

One of the kids caught his eye, and Luke turned away quickly. The last thing he needed was to look like a pedophile.

"Excuse me, Mister?" Luke lifted his head carefully. A dark-skinned boy, no older than ten years old, stood in front of him. He held a notebook in his bony arms. "Are you Detective Warren?"

"You can call me Luke." The Hunters had gathered a number of fans over the years. The children were Luke's favorites, especially now. They thought he was a superhero, just like in comic books and movies. He played along with the idea, not wishing to crush their dreams, although he did find it amusing. "What's your name?"

"Axel. Are you hurt?" The boy pointed timidly at the bandages around Luke's arm.

"What, this? It's no big deal."

"You're really brave. I wish I had powers like you." The boy clutched the notebook tighter.

Luke smiled. "You don't need powers to be brave, Axel. In fact, they're even a hassle sometimes."

"Axel!" A woman with wilted brown hair hurried toward them, her face strained in panic. She knelt beside the young boy and took his head between her hands. "You were supposed to stay by the games. What have I told you about running off?"

"Sorry, Ma."

The woman glanced toward Luke and Rae nonchalantly, then did a double take. Her eyebrows lifted high on her forehead, and her lips split into a smile. She extended her hand eagerly. "Hi, I'm Kay. Axel's mom." She shook Luke's hand, then Rae's, and looked at her son. "Did you get a signature?"

Axel lifted his notebook shyly. He opened it to a blank

page. "Will you sign this?"

"Of course." Luke took the pen that Kay offered him and jotted down a quick message, the same that he left for every child.

'Axel: Be brave, be strong, and most of all, don't give up hope—Luke.'

The little boy looked to Rae next, and she added her signature next to Luke's. Axel beamed widely and took back the notebook. Kay put her hand around his shoulder.

"Sweetheart, why don't you go back to play with the games? Mommy will hold the book for you."

Axel nodded eagerly and waved goodbye to Luke before dashing back toward the other children. Kay sat in the chair on Rae's left. Her face returned to its original tired look, which appeared to be permanent. "He has a brain tumor."

"Who, Axel?" Luke had only known the boy for a few minutes, but he had already made a close friend. Axel was only a child, the same age as the Dusk Walkers he would have to kill. His stomach twisted at the comparison.

Kay nodded. Her expression, as though she had used up all of her tears, was blank. "He won't last to the end of the year, according to the doctors."

"I'm so sorry," said Luke. What else could he say? She was about to lose her son, and she knew it. She had to watch him suffer, knowing he would not survive. Luke knew that if he were faced with the same situation, he would not be able to handle it. Kay looked spent to her last penny, but she still held strong.

"Thank you," said Kay. She glanced toward Axel, who pushed a toy train around wooden tracks. He looked healthy from a distance, despite the new information. "I should go to him."

"Of course." Luke gave her a smile as she stood and walked toward Axel. Kay touched her son's shoulder and motioned toward the exit. He dropped the train and took her hand as she led him out of the waiting room. Axel turned to give a quick wave to Luke before he disappeared completely from the latter's sight.

Luke turned back to Rae. His eyebrows knitted together when he saw that her expression was almost indifferent. "Are you okay?"

She shrugged. "I was just thinking. If you got so attached to that kid, what will happen when we find the Dusk Walkers?"

He stared at her in disbelief. "Even for you, that's cruel. You don't know Axel any more than I do. And he shouldn't have to die."

"People die every day, even children," said Rae, her eyes cold. "Axel's no different, and neither are the Dusk Walkers. I hope you realize that, because I can't have you chicken out when we get this job over with."

"I won't," said Luke. He grinded his teeth together, feeling a stronger anger toward her than he had in a long time. He turned away, staring back to where Axel and Kay had left. A surprise met him there: Gianna. She stood in the entranceway to the waiting room, clothed in an old pair of jeans and a flannel shirt. Her eyes searched the rows of faces, then found his. Her curious expression split into a smile as she hurried toward him and Rae.

Gianna kissed his cheek briefly, then sat in the chair in front of him. She straightened her glasses and glanced toward his bandages. "How's the arm?"

"Better now. How did you know we were here? This isn't the only hospital in the city."

"Phone. Technopath." She pointed at his pocket, where his phone resided, then at herself. "Your signal came from this hospital, so I drove here in hopes of meeting you two."

"You shouldn't have done that. It's dangerous, with the concussion and all."

Gianna scoffed. "It's just a headache. Besides, I've got news about the hunt."

"Me too. You go first."

"Jack is on the move. I don't know if the Dusk Walkers are with him, but he's leaving District Three."

"We'll follow him as soon as we're done here. My turn. First, the Dusk Walkers weren't alone when we went after them. A brother and sister were with him, both in their midteens. I have no clue who they were, but they were on Jack's side. Second, I told Roy about them. Get this." He lowered his voice to a whisper. They were not alone, and their subject was a risky one. "He said to kill them too."

"What?" exclaimed Gianna. Rae was silent.

"I know! I mean, killing five teens is bad enough, whether they've committed crimes or not. But two random kids…there's something not right about this," he said, voicing his recent thoughts.

"I'm with you. Something must have gone wrong in Roy's head when he learned about the attack on Vanessa." Gianna frowned. "So many kids getting hurt…this feels like a nightmare."

He thought of the first time they met. It had been a little less than a month after the Explosion. When he had woken, his amnesia had been so overwhelming that he had become a drunken mess, seeking shelter in a poor town on the outskirts of the city. Finally, Gianna found him. She was the first appointed Hunter. She had helped with Luke's rehabilitation and training, and in turn, Rae's as well. Gianna had been offered the position as leader of the team, but declined, and the role went to Luke.

Gianna looked at Rae, whose head was bowed in deep thought. "What's your opinion on the job? I can't remember if you said anything."

She shrugged. "We do what we have to do."

"That's your answer? You're okay with murdering seven kids?"

"This isn't murder," said Rae. "It's vermin extermination."

CHAPTER FIFTEEN

The Dusk Walkers preferred to steal food from District Two, where the small independent stores had good stock, unlike in District Three. However, Jack was used to roaming the streets in the early morning, when fewer people were around. Now, before midnight, the sidewalks were bustling with late-night shoppers. Jack kept his eye and ears open for any signs of suspicion. It was likely that, following his escape, the news had yet again forcefully engraved his face into everybody's minds.

In front of an antiques store, he sat on a bench that was occupied by a man reading a newspaper aloud to himself.

"The one-year anniversary of the Oktoberfest massacre is tomorrow…" said the man.

Jack ignored him and zipped his bag open to dig around the bottom until he found a pair of sunglasses. After he put them on and pulled up his hood, he was harder to recognize, blending in with the rest of the nobodies who populated the streets.

He walked down the sidewalk, and no one looked twice at him. They did not know that he marched to his death. It was a normal evening for them, the lucky bastards. The lady in front of him, with a 1960s haircut and a leopard-patterned jacket, would surely survive the night. So would the two men who exited the fast-food restaurant across the street holding hands. They would not care if Jack died. In fact, they might celebrate, as most of the city would.

Initially, after a failed attempt to use the Dusk Walkers' parents to reason with them, the military had been involved in chasing down the kids. Helicopters and authorities were set at the borders of every District, monitoring who crossed over. The Dusk Walkers had hidden in the sewers for a week.

Almost a year after the Explosion, the new mayor had been idiotic enough to send the authorities away. As soon as the Hunters came into the picture, he had deemed the three young adults more capable than the United States Army. The military had obliged, with little interest in the troublemakers at the time. From what Jack had heard from the rumor mill, negotiations were in the making among the police department, the mayor, and the governor himself. So far, there was no verdict on the replacement of the Hunters, but Jack would never know the ending. He could only hope that his friends would be safe while he was gone.

"They'd better catch that Turner boy soon!"

Jack froze. The voice came from in front of an electronics store that showcased televisions in the window. An old lady with wispy white hair stood in front of the window, her wrinkly, hooded nose almost touching the glass.

"I'm telling you, in my days, the authorities weren't nearly this soft. Heck, those Hunters should be locked up too! They give me the shivers."

"Oh, come on, Gram," said a young man, whose hair was impossibly thick, as though a little orange dog had crawled onto the top of his head and died there. "They're doing their best. At least feel bad for Gabriel Turner."

"Why should I? How could he live with himself after raising that child scum?"

Gabriel Turner? That was his father's name. He recognized it from his interrogation with Roy. Jack ignored the insult and wondered why the old woman's grandson spoke of his dad as though something had happened.

"Move over, Carrottop," said Jack, trying to get a look at the displays.

A newscaster spoke quickly, but the sound was muted. However, captions appeared and disappeared at the bottom of the screen. When a video clip aired instead of the announcer's face, the words continued to materialize. He saw the aftermath of a car crash. Two completely wrecked vehicles blocked a section of a major highway. Firefighters hosed down the flames.

No casualties have been reported, but four individuals have been critically injured, including Gabriel Turner, father of seventeen-year-old Jack Turner, who is still at large after his recent escape from the NYPD.

"If they don't catch him soon, I'm moving back to

Chicago!"

"Would you calm down, Gram?"

"Oh fine," said the elderly lady. "Let's go, they're just repeating the same thing they said five minutes ago." Carrottop and his grandmother continued walking, and Jack had the TVs to himself. The newscaster was back, a picture of the crash in the corner of the screen.

The four injured civilians were safely transported to the nearest hospital. We wish them a speedy recovery.

The nearest hospital. Considering the location of the accident, the hospital was within walking distance. As the newscaster changed the subject, Jack chewed on his lower lip. Should he go speak to his father, to at least see what he was like? The fact that Gabriel had been to jail for child abuse did not disturb him. Captain Roy could have lied, or the story could have been exaggerated. Even if it wasn't, he did not care. In the hospital, a wounded Gabriel could not hurt him. He decided that he should get something useful done before his death. Meeting his father would present some kind of closure. Yes, he would do that. If the Hunters caught up with him there and killed him, that was fine. The ordeal would be over with.

Jack returned to the bench where he had put on his sunglasses. This time he retrieved a creased map of the city from his backpack. Sure enough, the hospital he searched for was a mere five blocks away.

Fifteen minutes later, he was inside the building.

"Do you have any identification?" The hospital

receptionist's hair was pinned up as tightly as her personality.

"Not mine, no. Look lady, I already told ya. My dad needed me to check on Gabe Turner, but he's sick, and my ma's workin' late, so he sent me," said Jack in his best Brooklyn accent.

The receptionist was not convinced. "Why didn't he just come in by himself?"

"Like I said, he's got the flu. Wouldn't be so smart for him to come to a place full o' sick people, would it?"

She blinked slowly. "Give me your dad's ID."

"That, I can do!" He smiled, handing her a doctor's identification badge that he had nicked from a man leaving the hospital in a hurry. It was possible that he had been ill, but Jack could not know for sure.

The woman glanced at it, then back to Jack. "Take off the glasses."

He glanced quickly around the room. No one appeared able to take him down at a moment's notice. Now that he thought about it, the receptionist might have been sitting at her desk for at least a few hours, directing people up and down the floors. She might not have seen the news that Jack Turner had escaped from prison. He could risk it. If she showed any sign of recognition, he would run before she could call security on him. He bit his lip and pulled off his shades.

She looked from him to the little picture of the doctor

on the badge. "I don't see the family resemblance," she said, still staring at the photo of the gaunt Asian man.

"Well, folks are always sayin' how much I look like my ma." He threw in a persuasive grin as the cherry on top.

She glared suspiciously at him, then noticed the growing waiting line behind him. "Fine, go. If I hear one word about you causing trouble, I'm calling security."

"Thank you, kind lady!" He beamed, putting his sunglasses back on. "Whouldja mind tellin' me what room Gabriel Turner is in, while you're at it?"

A couple quick clicks of her mouse later, the receptionist had his answer. "Ward 431. Now get out of my sight."

Jack sighed airily as he walked toward the elevator. "Oh, if only all the women in the universe were as kind as you, ma'am." He darted off before she could react, unable to believe his luck. Somehow, by a miracle perhaps, she had not recognized him. Either she was too busy trying to identify him as the doctor's son, or she never checked the news. He stopped thinking and took the elevator to the fourth floor.

"You said Gabriel is your uncle?" Jack and Doctor George Fremont walked down the hall toward Jack's father's ward. He had introduced himself as Robert Hatfield, a name he had come up with on the spot. "We looked for the next of kin, but we only found his son, of course."

"Actually he's my second cousin twice removed, or something like that. It's a big family," lied Jack. "I just heard about the crash. How's he doing?"

"Not good. He's sustained several contusions, blood loss, a mild concussion, and…" Doctor Fremont trailed off.

"And what?"

"The crash impaired his sight. If he survives, he won't see again," said the doctor.

Jack paused mid-nod. "If he survives?"

"He isn't accepting medication. Something about God's will." They stopped walking in front of a closed ward, number 431. He tried to take a glance inside, but the blinds were tightly shut. "I'll leave you here, then." The doctor turned and continued on his way down the hall, leaving Jack outside his father's room.

He hesitated before opening the door, not even sure of what he was doing. What might be one of the last events of his life was to visit his father, the man who had beaten him for seven years of his childhood. It made no sense. Jack had acted on impulse, as he always had.

"Screw it." He turned the doorknob and entered ward 431. The walls were completely blank, and the curtains were all drawn over the windows. The room had an overall cold feeling to it. His attention shifted to the man who lay on the bed, still as water.

Gabriel was not the most attractive man in the city.

His large belly was a massive bump under the thin bed sheets. His head was bald and shiny, his eyebrows were like fat black caterpillars on his flat face, and his neck was almost nonexistent.

I must have gotten my good looks from my mom, thought Jack. If he remembered correctly, Erin Turner had died of cancer when her son was seven years old, when Gabriel had lost his mind.

"Who's there?" The injured man opened his unseeing eyes. They were precisely the same color as Jack's.

"Call me Bob." Jack modified his alias' first name.

"You a doctor, Bob?" Gabriel turned toward Jack, his eyes staring at the air inches to the right of his shoulder.

"Uh…no, not really."

"Good. No one can save me."

"Why not? The doctors here are fine, and they could make you better if you didn't refuse their medication." Jack gave an encouraging smile, although Gabriel could not see him. He wanted his father to recognize him. He wanted to see a sign that the man cared at all.

"I've done some bad things, Bob. Things that can't be forgiven. Now I've been punished."

"What do you mean?"

"The crash. Maybe I'm not supposed to live. Maybe it was God's will."

Jack did not often think about religion. It had not occurred to him that his father might have strong views about the subject. Jack did not believe in a higher power. If God existed, why did he hate the Dusk Walkers so much? They had done nothing so wrong as to deserve the injustice they experienced.

"Bob, get my bag for me." It was not a request that Gabriel spoke. It was an order. Jack lifted the heavy backpack onto the hospital bed. "There's a picture in the front pocket. Give it to me."

He decided not to question why a blind man wanted a picture, and he searched anyway. The front pocket of the bag held a full keychain, a wallet, and a ballpoint pen. He almost told Gabriel that the picture was not there, then he felt a smooth surface at the bottom of the pocket and pulled it out. It was a four-by-six-inch photo, torn and folded many times. Under the coffee stain in one corner, Jack could distinguish a good-looking woman with beautiful, long hair. Although she smiled, there was a cold, sad look permanently etched onto her face. It was visible in her dark eyes, tiny in the picture. She held a small boy in her arms, who was no older than six. His auburn hair, exactly the same shade as his mother's, reached his shoulders. Unlike the woman who embraced him, he grinned vibrantly, unaware of any problems in the world. The two of them stood on the porch of an old house that wouldn't even look good with a paint job. Jack assumed this was him and Erin, after she had been diagnosed with cancer.

After a moment of staring at his and his mother's faces, Jack handed the picture to his father. Gabriel took it with trembling, sausage-like fingers. "That's her...Erin. My beautiful Erin." Gabriel choked beneath a sob.

Jack noticed that he was not mentioned in any way, but he did not bring that up. There was no need to provoke him.

"Bob, why are you here? You're not a doctor...what do you want?"

"I—I, umm..." He shot a quick glance around the room, and upon finding nothing to help him, he looked back at his father. "I dunno. Nothing, really."

Somehow, Gabriel got hold of the front of Jack's sweater and pulled his son close to him. "So what the hell are you doing here?" Gabriel struggled for air. "Get out now."

"Yeah, okay, I will. But you need to calm down," said Jack. The beeps of the heart monitor behind him increased in speed, as did his own heartbeats.

His father did not care. A large hand pulled a chain out of Jack's shirt: the blank army tags. Jack realized that maybe he had worn the tags long before the Explosion. They could have been from his parents. "Jack...I thought that I'd never see you again."

That was when Gabriel Turner took his last breath, the faintest smile on his face as he held the picture of his wife and son in one hand, and Jack's army tags in the other, the chain still around Jack's neck.

The heart monitor produced a flat tone, and Jack

realized that doctors would arrive at any moment. He slipped his head out from the chain, leaving the tags in his father's clenched fist. Meeting his father had been nothing but odd. The man was a stranger to him. No closure had been offered. The visit had only raised more questions in Jack's mind. Did Gabriel love him? Did he regret hurting Jack? Did he really want to die, as his son would later that night? Jack could only stand there and stare at the motionless body.

It wasn't long before a group of doctors, including Doctor Fremont, ran in to attempt to revive Gabriel. Jack knew they did not have a chance. His father was dead.

"Who're you?" said a middle-aged nurse after she pushed past him to get to her patient.

"Turner." Jack backed out the door that had been left ajar. "Jack Turner."

CHAPTER SIXTEEN

Jack made sure that his hood was on his head and that his glasses would not fall off his nose. He headed down the hall, staring at the white tiles in front of him, the same questions repeating themselves in his mind.

"Hey, you!" As he walked around the corner, he caught a glimpse of two burly police officers on his tail. He groaned, slapping a hand to his forehead. The receptionist must have warned security that he was in Gabriel's room. He had suspected that the entire situation was too perfect for her to not have recognized him. "Stop!"

Jack sprinted down the hall, dodging flabbergasted doctors on his way to the nearest window. His hood fell back, then he was nearly trapped in an IV carousel. People attempted to stop him once they realized who he was. It was time to do something that he had wanted to try again for a long time, but he was on the fourth floor. It was too high. Then, out of pure luck, he came upon a door that led to the staircase. He glanced behind him; the officers were gaining on him. He leapt down the stairs four or five at a time, arriving at the next floor in seconds, still too high to risk it. He jumped down the next flight of stairs when he knew that he could not risk another floor.

Short of breath, he burst through the door that led to the second-floor corridor. He slammed it shut behind him, and for a fraction of a second he thought he could make a break for it. But the hinges were on the other side of the door. One of the officers pulled it open as soon as he let go of the handle. A quick glance behind him let Jack know that the other man was on the same floor, racing toward him.

Jack threw his fist at the first officer's nose. He sucked in a quick breath in a wince, feeling both the bones in the officer's nose and the bones in his own hand crack. Jack raced down the hall with the other officer on his tail. This was his chance. When he came to the end of the corridor, he broke into his fastest sprint and dived shoulder-first through the fragile glass. It did not break easily, but putting all of his weight into it caused the window to shatter.

Jack landed in the bushes, and his left wrist snapped, sending a blinding jolt of pain through his arm. The glass had cut his face and hands, but it was nothing to cry about. He looked to the second-floor window. Both police officers, one sporting a bloody nose, leaned out of the opening.

"Ha!" Jack laughed off his discomfort as he walked toward the street. "Beat that, suckers!"

The bones in his wrist grinded back into place, and he cradled it gingerly while it healed. He thought of how the others would react if he told them about his stunt. Lily and Alix would eat it up, while Cordy and Eva would almost certainly roll their eyes. Ever since he had broken his arm by jumping from a first-storey window years ago, he had always wanted to try again and succeed. The smile vanished when he remembered that he would never tell the story to his friends, nor anything else in his lifetime.

A car door slammed shut several times in a row. Jack whirled around and saw that the sound did not originate from a vehicle, but from the police officers in the window. They had drawn their handguns and shot at him. From that distance, their aim was weak, though there was always the chance that they would get lucky and hit their target. Even though he wandered around District Two in the purpose of letting himself get killed, he would rather die by Luke's hand than to get shot in the back by stunt cop number two. He ran, darting between parked ambulances until he was able to turn a corner so that he was no longer in the line of fire.

When his adrenaline wore off, he was able to think properly. He began by acting as though he belonged there, on the never-ending sidewalk alongside a shopping outlet. Jack breathed slowly in and out, becoming lost in his thoughts. The Hunters could be there at any moment, and he wanted to be ready when they were. He planned to put up a small fight that he could never win, and that would be it.

It seemed too simple when it was put that way. He did not want to leave his friends. He did not want to die. He wanted to be free. He wanted to survive, in a world where the Hunters could not follow him. There was no theory that would make that possible.

The streets cleared when he left the main roads of District Two. He took a shortcut through a park that would soon be demolished. The grass had died, and the trees withered. The pavement was cracked under his feet, and he had to skip around the potholes in fear of tripping.

As he arrived at the exit on the other side of the park, he tapped his knuckles against the fence, the cold metal numbing his fingers. He gripped the pole and swung his body around until he was outside of the park. The sight that awaited him froze his blood in its tracks, and his jaw dropped.

"Don't move!"

A quick count revealed nearly ten semiautomatics aimed at him, wielded by police officers who stood behind their vehicles. They were parked in a half circle around the fence, forming a barrier. Luke was not among them, nor were Gianna or Rae.

"Hands up, Turner," said an officer, his brow glistening with sweat in the lamplight.

Jack's fingers trembled at his sides. It took a great effort to keep breathing. He had three options: to surrender, which was never a true option for him, to fight his way past the cops, which never ended well, or to turn around and run back through the park.

He chose to run. He would throw an insult at the officers for good measure, then turn on his heels and flee, taking strides long enough to strain his muscles as he struggled for control over his heartbeat. He would get as far away from these jerks as he could. He would find the Hunters.

But his feet would not budge. Jack remained on the sidewalk on the edge of the park, time as frozen as his body. The police officers must have followed him from the hospital, or other people had tipped them off. He had not been careful in disguising himself. He forced himself to breathe, to get oxygen to his brain in order for his muscles to move.

Run. With the encouragement of his mind, he was able to dig the toes of his sneakers into the cracked cement of the sidewalk, and he pushed forward with his stronger leg. Jack lifted his twin limb to take the second giant step, almost throwing himself down the slope instead of running. He soon gathered speed. The officers did not follow him. That was the opposite of what they were supposed to do. Jack paused midrun, and his breath hitched when he saw what fate had decided for him now.

Two men had drawn rifles. The barrels now clicked into place. He felt the first shot before he heard it. "Argh!" Jack stumbled backward, tripping over his own feet until he regained his balance. He pressed his fingers to his side and saw blood. It would heal in minutes, and he could still run. He continued his race toward the other end of the park, drawing short, shallow breaths. His legs felt as though they were gelatin.

Two more police cars were parked at the second entrance. An officer stepped out, gun raised at Jack, who slowed to a stop. He looked back to the first set of officers up the hill. He was trapped. He panted, his lungs fighting for the air they needed. Black spots appeared at the corners of his eyes. He blinked and began to lift his hands above his head.

Another blast behind him, louder than the shotgun, rang through the air. It was immediately followed by a sudden and sharp pain just above his knee. Jack yelled and collapsed, his elbows breaking his fall. A groan escaped his lips, his face pressed into the dry grass. His leg jerked underneath him, and he reminded himself that he would heal soon. That dulled the pain slightly and made it worse all at once.

The officer from the foot of the hill walked toward him, stowing away his pistol. Jack reached toward the knife at his belt. If he healed on time, perhaps he could still make a run for it. He did not want to be killed in a jail cell like a fish in a barrel. His fingers brushed the handle of his weapon, then a boot pressed down on his hand. The officer leaned his weight onto Jack's fingers until he pulled away.

Jack let out a shaky gasp, tears forming by themselves in his eyes. The officer took Jack's knife, then pressed the barrel of the pistol to the back of the boy's head. The gun was still warm.

"I could put you down right now and save the Hunters some trouble. They don't seem to be doing a very good job of keeping you under control. Where are they now, for starters? I was called because Warren couldn't be reached. What was so important that kept him from doing his only job?"

Jack struggled to free himself, but his weak thrashing was useless. The officers from the top and the bottom of the hill approached. "Killing him wouldn't do any of us good," said one of them. "We kill him, and the other Dusk Walkers disappear forever."

"Wise words," said Jack, his voice hoarse. The first officer glared at him, and Jack only smiled, relieved that his leg was beginning to heal. He was released, but he only had a moment to stretch his sore limbs before two officers pulled him to his feet and marched him down the hill toward the vehicles. His knife was in the clutches of the officer with the pistol. Jack did a mental review of his healed injuries: a shotgun blast had gotten him under his ribs, his leg had been shot, and he had been shoved around to the officers' pleasure. These men were not nearly as considerate as the authorities he had met in the past.

His point was proven when Jack was slammed against the police car at the bottom of the hill, the door handle banging against his hip. He was patted down, but the only weapon he had been carrying was his knife. When they turned him around, sharp handcuffs were tightened around his wrists, and the officers guided him into the backseat. The officer in control slid into the passenger seat while another drove. Jack gave a heavy sigh and leaned back. How would he escape this time?

He scowled, stumped, and said nothing.

He was silent during the entire trip to the police station, which was different from the Hunters' building. This one was a stocky, rectangular building with beige and grey sides to each wall. A great blue garage stood out from the rest of the structure, the number of the precinct marked in bold white letters on the front. They drove around the back of the building, where they slowed to a stop in a parking spot near the backdoor. Jack looked behind him. The rest of the squadron parked alongside them.

Two officers gripped both his arms and hauled him out of the vehicle, while another walked ahead to open the door to the building. The rest followed them through the precinct, only a few officers remaining to lead Jack to the holding cells. There were two cages. A couple of people were already inside one of them, but he could not see their faces quite yet.

"Aren't you supposed to do other things before putting me in here? Get a detention authorization, tell me my Miranda rights, PACE codes, etcetera?" said Jack.

"Not for you, Turner. You're a very special case," said a thin man with hollowed cheeks, clapping him on his back. Jack could see his teeth moving under his skin. He gave a weak smile.

"We'll put him in the second cell." A policewoman advanced to the front of the line now, her penciled eyebrows stern and her black hair in a tight bun. As Jack approached the cell, he could see the two men better. They sat on a bench against the back wall, both burly with questionable hygiene. Jack recognized one of them.

He forced himself to not look directly at Zephyr, the broad-shouldered, shaved-head member of the Nor'easters. The policewoman unlocked the second cell door and guided Jack inside. He was quiet as he sat on the bench, only feet away from Zephyr. Instead of speaking, Jack listened to what the officers said to each other.

"As much as I would love to smack the kid down with

the hand of God in a proper trial, Captain Roy insists that the Hunters deal with him themselves," said the woman.

"Psst, Turner." Zephyr inched toward Jack on the bench. Jack pressed his finger to his own lips, straining his ears to hear.

"If we're waiting on the Hunters, what's taking them so long? I thought Warren was supposed to be fast," said a male officer.

"No one can get in contact with them at the moment. Captain Roy's left to look for them." The Hunters were nowhere to be found. Maybe Jack would be lucky enough to escape his death once more. No, he could not think that way. He could not consider that option, which would imply that he wanted to run for the rest of his life. He was tired of running.

"Zephyr," said Jack finally, moving toward the taller man. "Where are the rest of you?"

"Who, Squall and the rest, ya mean? Naw, man. I was too slow, so I got caught." Zephyr leaned closer. "But get this: Cyclone was the one who called the coppers in the first place. He ditched us before we even knew what was going on."

"No way. The new guy?" Jack tried to act surprised, discovering that he was not. Cyclone had hated the Dusk Walkers from the beginning. Before their meeting, Cyclone had alerted the police. It did not seem worthy of a gang member to call upon the authorities, but neither did defying one's superiors.

Zephyr nodded.

"What a dick."

"Turner," said the policewoman. "Got something to say?"

Jack scoffed. "Well, you know, we were just wondering…you seem kinda moody. We thought it might be menopause."

She clenched her jaw, and a vein bulged from her neck. She turned back to her colleagues. "The best we can do for now is to keep him locked up. You watch him." She tossed a set of keys to another officer, and she walked away, accompanied by the rest of the officers. Their footsteps disappeared into the noise of the chatter in the main office.

Lifting a hand to shield his mouth from the onlookers, Jack whispered to Zephyr, "Distract them. I'll bust you out later."

"No way in hell."

"This is important. I can't waste my time here." Jack had reconsidered his options. He would die tonight, that was certain. However, he would not die in a holding cell with his hands cuffed in front of him. He would not give Luke that pleasure.

"Oh, and you think I can?" Zephyr stood, coming up to at least a head taller than Jack. "D'ya think you're better than me?"

Jack shrugged, standing up as well. "What if I do?"

Zephyr slammed his fist against the chain-link wall that separated them. "Then I'll kick your ass."

"Go right ahead."

"Break it up in there!" said the thin officer.

The hulking man with more tattoos than bare skin climbed to his feet. "Shut your mouth, Dusk Walker."

"That's enough!" The officer went to open the door to the first cell, but it opened before he could even reach it. As did Jack's cell.

Jack slipped past the door without a second of hesitation. Arms wrapped around his waist, lifting him off the ground. Jack tried to kick the officer's legs, then his eyes landed on something below him: a ring of keys. Grinning widely, he thrust out his hand and snatched the ring from the officer's belt. The officer's attention was on Zephyr and the tattooed man.

Jack slashed the officer's hand with the sharpest key, drawing blood. The officer yelled, his grip loosened, and Jack dashed through the door, sliding it shut behind him. He glanced at the cop and the two inmates, who still fought.

When he turned around, two guns were pointed at his chest, held by a couple of officers who looked significantly more serious than the others he had encountered that night. They would not allow Jack to escape so easily. Now aware of the cruelty of some police officers, he did not doubt they would shoot him. It was a risk he would have to take.

Jack dashed around the two officers. Out of the corner of his eye, he saw them pull the triggers. Only a couple of empty clicks were produced. The guns were jammed. While the officers paused, perplexed, Jack took the opportunity to run. He did not ask himself what had happened to the triggers. He only gripped the keys tightly in his hands. He needed to retrieve his knife and release himself from the handcuffs.

He rushed past closed doors, twisting from left to right for a place to hide. Footsteps down the hall approached, and a door snapped open to his right. He leapt backward in surprise, but no one exited the room. Jack was only briefly confused before he wrenched open the door and swung it shut behind him. When he saw that no one was inside, he pressed his ear to the door in order to hear what was occurring outside. It was difficult to make out the words, for his heart hammered so loudly that he feared it could be heard on the other side of the door.

"There's a riot on Tenth Avenue," said one officer to another. "A protest gone bad. There was some sort of technical issue that sent the whole thing spinning out of control. They need as many hands as they can get. The Hunters can take care of Turner when they get here."

They still did not know that Jack had escaped the holding cell. This was his opportunity to escape. He could do it. He selected the smallest key on the ring and unlocked his handcuffs. He whirled around and examined his surroundings. Cabinets stood against the walls of the room, with a desk at the center. Three evidence bags lay on the wooden desk. In the first was his knife. He took his weapon and slid it into his belt. Upon casting a quick gaze at the other two bags, his face split into a mad grin. He still needed to attract Luke's attention.

He pocketed a half-empty matchbox from one bag and a small tube of lighter fluid from the other before leaving the room.

Jack glanced from side to side, listening for any sounds in the empty hall. He looked upward. A security camera was pointed at him. Now that he was armed, he had gained a significant amount of confidence, as well as adrenaline. They would both help him that night. He stared back at the camera. If it moved, that meant they were watching him. It remained immobile.

Not all of the officers in the precinct could be at the riot. Some of them had to have remained at the station, and someone should have noticed that he was on his way to escaping. Still, no one came after him.

Jack staggered backward and shielded his face with his arms when snapping sounds and sparks came from the camera. It had moved, but not in the way that he had expected. He lowered his arms. The camera was broken

The camera was not the only broken piece of technology. The florescent light above his head blinked out as well. All the lights in the hallway went black one after the other. This was not William's doing. He was incapable of physically breaking lamps and could only manipulate the light particles in the air. Someone else was toying with the lights. A faded glow came from the windows that lit his way, along with a strange red radiance from around the corner. Jack stiffened. Perhaps he was imagining it.

As he walked forward, only hearing his trembling breaths, he could feel his heartbeat accelerate once more. The red light could be anything. It could be a sniper's aim, or a glowing fairy with wings. It could also be an exit sign, which he discovered when he turned the corner. Below the neon words was the emergency exit door.

"Gianna," he muttered, realizing what he was in the middle of. The technopath had been leading him out of the building the whole time. She had unlocked the doors and stopped the guns. She broke the lights. "Thanks...I think."

It was after he spoke that he understood. If he left the building, Luke, Gianna, and Rae awaited him. If he remained, the other officers would intercept him.

The exit sign flashed almost insistently. Voices echoed from the center of the building. Luke would find him whether he left or he stayed. Jack leaned into the heavy door, still preferring a death where he went down fighting. It opened under his touch, and streetlamps lit the night outside. He glanced from side to side, searching the parking lot for silhouettes. He detected nothing.

He needed to throw the more incompetent officers off his scent. He assumed that Gianna had taken out all the security cameras to disorient his attackers, which had given him the time that he needed. Now he only needed to attract the Hunters' attention, and he had exactly the right tools for the job.

He jogged up a small slope until he arrived in front of a row of cars in the middle of the street. He selected the oldest-looking model, a shabby blue Ford. If the Hunters would not come to him, he would have to bring them his way. Jack tugged off his sweater and rolled it around his elbow as he approached the blue car. Acting swiftly, he swung his arm into the passenger-seat window. It shattered, and the alarm blared until he could hear no more. Jack shook off the glass and drew a deep breath. "Luke!"

He had not even heard his own voice in his ears because the alarm was too loud. He blinked tears of frustration from his eyes when he saw no one.

"Fine." He pulled the sweater back on and drew the lighter fluid and the matchbox. Sticking his hand through the window, he splashed some of the liquid onto the seat. It was not enough, so he dropped the bottle inside. He took a match from the box and struck a single flame. He reached back through the broken window and let go.

The fire spread slowly at first, licking the synthetic leather of the seats before catching onto the velvety floor pads. Jack turned away from the flames. Vandalism and arson were part of his reputation. He might as well live up to the expectations of the city before he died.

A shriek cut through the air. Smoke and heat blinded him when he searched for the source.

"Jack!" His name was called, not by Luke's deep pitch, nor by Gianna or Rae's feminine tones, but by a familiar shrill. Alix.

CHAPTER SEVENTEEN

Jack whirled around, squinting to see her. She stood near the highway, a flashlight illuminating her frantic eyes, like a deer frozen in the headlights of a car. None other than Luke wielded the source of light.

"No..." His voice was a breath, no more than a whisper.

A low rumble rose behind him, and warmth heated the back of his neck. Jack turned and saw that the fire had spread. It would soon reach the fuel tank, which meant that he had to be gone. At least he had gotten Luke's attention.

The backdoor to the police station burst open, and Jack's breath caught in his throat. He was once again faced with the choice of being caught by the cops or being killed by Luke. This time, Alix's life was at risk, and the decision was easier to make than before.

Luke ran, his body a blur, although not as quick as usual. The child he carried slowed him down. Jack knew what the plan was; he wasn't that stupid. Luke would use Alix as bait to lure him to a secluded area, where he would kill them both. Jack did not care. He followed his enemy. Shots fired from behind, and he hardly paid attention. Luke was his priority now.

Jack reached the highway, crossing the lanes at his greatest speed. Drivers honked their horns at him, not even noticing Luke. Jack ignored them, only taking his eyes off the fleeing figures to make sure he did not trip over the curb. Two officers were on his tail, determined to catch him for good. They were persistent. Jack was even more so.

He turned corners when Luke did, and his lungs strained, but it did not matter. He had given himself up in order to protect Alix and the others, and he would not let that sacrifice be in vain. If she had followed him when he left the bungalow, he would scold her later for doing so, if he could. For now, he would have to live long enough to get to her.

They had sprinted at least three blocks when Luke slowed down. The two officers were gone. Space-themed graffiti lined the walls, and panels of wood were stacked in towers behind a fence. There was a passageway between two buildings in the back that led to an unknown destination. Jack's breath left his throat in short wheezes. He clutched at the cramp in his side, grasping at the fence with his other hand. He blinked his dry eyes rapidly.

Luke's breathing had hardly been affected. He stood near a tower of panels, his arm around Alix's waist. Her eyes were full of panic, unharmed at the moment. She was terrified, unable to think of the obvious action to take. *Come on, Al. Use your fire. Hurt him.* He wanted to shout those words at her, but he could not gather enough oxygen to project his voice.

Jack's angry glower met Luke's almost curious stare. There was a certain stillness about the Hunter, whose lips parted and eyes softened. He could have been sad, or guilty about having to kill the Dusk Walkers. Jack scoffed and abandoned the thought. Luke was a killer, of blood colder than the winters of Canada.

His denial was proved reasonable when Luke departed once more through the gap between two buildings. Jack only got one look at Alix, whose face was shiny with tears. He would save her before he died. That was the promise he made himself.

Nevertheless, Jack could not run anymore. His adrenaline left him. He combed back his windswept hair with his fingers, and sweat pooled on his face and under his arms. Despite the inconveniences, he managed to put one foot in front of the other, making slow progress. He started into a jog before building up speed.

Then he was on his back, at a loss for what could have put him there. He traced back his steps. There had been an impact against his chest, sharp and hard, although he had seen nothing. It sent a jolt of pain through his body. It knocked all the breath out of his struggling lungs, and he could not move. It was as though a great weight, like a boulder or an elephant, sat atop his chest. He tried to sit up and found that he was incapable of doing so. Even rolling onto his side was impossible.

"It's like an air gun, just with a wider diameter and range."

Gianna. She and Rae approached him, arriving from the same passageway that Luke had taken. Gianna knelt beside him, a large rifle in her hands. Jack looked at it more carefully and saw that it was too stout to be a rifle.

"Basically, it's less flimsy pellets and more…science fiction," said Gianna. She pushed her glasses up the bridge of her nose, smiling triumphantly. "I made it myself."

Jack wheezed deeply and tried to sit up once more, but Gianna put a hand on his shoulder.

"Careful, sweetie, you'll hurt yourself. The effects will wear off soon. You might have a few cracked ribs, but you're safe, and you can heal properly."

"You…the police station…" He winced. The words were hardly coherent. It hurt to speak.

"I helped you out so that Luke could lead you here, yes. We couldn't walk in and kill you in front of all those cops. They don't know about our new orders. And we can't kill you here, either. Too many people around. They would hear a pistol."

"Nice job, partner," said Rae, crossing her arms over her purple jacket. "Why don't you just go ahead and tell him your whole life story while you're at it? Quit chatting, we gotta go."

Gianna pulled a piece of folded paper out of her pocket. "Meet us here. We couldn't have you chasing Luke all the way across the city, so this is our pit stop. Get to the written location before sunrise. That's where

Alix will be." She put the paper into Jack's hand and folded his fingers over it.

"Wait," gasped Jack when they turned to follow Luke.

Gianna looked down at him, the gun hanging loosely at her side. He saw the same look of pity on her face that Luke had worn. Rae only gave a heavy sigh, tapping her foot impatiently.

"Please, just…don't hurt her. Don't hurt Al…please." That was a word that rarely escaped his mouth, especially to his enemies. Jack made a point of never asking for mercy, and it would be one of his final words. He hoped the Hunters would see that and spare his youngest friend. "Don't—"

"Oh, shut it, filth." Rae glared at him like he were a piece of gum stuck on her best shoe, or worse. She tugged on Gianna's arm. "Let's go."

The brunette stood her ground, her eyelids fluttering rapidly in shock. Her mouth dropped open a few times before she uttered three small words. "I'm so sorry."

He closed his eyes. Despite Gianna's compassion, the Hunters would carry through with their mission. They would still kill Alix after he died. "No, please…" He clenched his fists around the paper in his hand, the edges biting into his palm. Rae took Gianna's arm once more, and they left, the sounds of their footsteps masked by sirens. The noise was distant. The police cars were at least two blocks away, and the sirens began to fade. The officers were no longer a threat to him. His full attention was now on finding Alix.

Curling his fingers around the coils of the fence, he dragged himself off of the damp asphalt and into a standing position. His torso ached, but it was easier to breathe in an upright position, and he sucked in deep gulps of air until he was calm.

He unfolded Gianna's paper and read the address. The street name was unfamiliar, so he would have to locate it first. His first thought was to steal a map of the city from a convenience store, then he laughed. They lived in the age of computers. Manually scanning a paper map for a single street name would take hours, which he and Alix did not have. The libraries were closed, so he would not be able to use a computer there.

He would have to do what he did best: steal.

The streets were not crowded at that time of night, although some hunched-over figures passed him on the sidewalk. Jack had his hood up, but his sunglasses and backpack had been lost upon his arrest. He would only have to be more cautious.

He advanced at a leisurely pace, remembering his friends' smiles, his mind lingering a little longer on Eva's. He would miss them. His hands started to shake, and he stuffed them into his pockets as if that would make them stop. He cherished the breaths of polluted air that he took, which were some of his last.

Ahead of him, a short man with curly black hair and a straight black coat walked his way. The man's eyes were fixed on his phone. Jack slowed his steps and glanced around them. They were the only ones on the block for as far as he could see. "Hi."

The man stopped and frowned at him, at the boy with the blood on his clothes and a mischievous look in his eyes. His bushy eyebrows raised in confusion. "Do I know you?"

"I hope not," said Jack. "Can I borrow your phone?"

"Piss off." The man wrapped his fingers around the device protectively and attempted to walk past Jack, who drew his knife.

"Can I borrow it now?" He raised the blade to eye level, and the man's face went white as he backed against the wall outside the parking garage. It was not the same building where Jack had been arrested the other day, although they were similar. A different company owned this one, and its fees were much cheaper than the first.

"Th—that is brand new," sputtered the man as he handed over the phone. "It's office-issued. It isn't even mine!"

Jack stuck out his bottom lip in a pout and patted the man's shoulder. "I actually meant it when I said that I'm going to borrow it. I just need to check something."

Jack found the map application on the phone and typed in the address from Gianna's paper. It was in District Two, only blocks away from Prospect Park. He knew how to get there.

"Thanks."

"You're...welcome?" The man with the coat took his phone back with stubby fingers. Jack flashed a quick smile before dashing off toward his destination.

It would take much too long to get there on foot, and he did not trust public transportation without the company of his fellow Dusk Walkers. There were too many people in a confined area, and he could be overpowered easily if recognized. He would have to find another way to get there.

Since there were no other people on the block, he would have to keep walking. He could not steal a car, since only Eva had ever jumpstarted one for him. That was her responsibility. He pulled up a memory of her early moments behind the wheel.

Years before, he had sat in the passenger seat of a stolen car while Eva drove. She had gotten the hang of it very quickly, despite a few occasions where she drove through a red light. Once they had reached a highway, they had encouraged her to go as fast as she could. It was not long before police sirens alerted them to the presence of the authorities, but she had continued to drive. They had almost been cornered when more officers arrived and set up road spikes ahead. However, Lily had flown out of the car in her eagle form. She morphed back into a human and moved the spikes out of the way, then flew back through the open window. Eventually, the Dusk Walkers had abandoned the car and had escaped the police officers without a scratch.

Jack smiled at the details he remembered from that day: his and Cordy's shouts of encouragement, the thrum of the helicopter above their heads, Lily's laughter as she returned from the outside, a strand of hair caught between Eva's lips...

He cleared his throat. He could not waste his time on memories. They would hurt him more than dying, now that he knew that he would never see his friends again. At least he could say goodbye to Alix. That would at least be some comfort.

Jack continued to walk at a steady pace, his knife in his belt, until he reached a street with a children's park. He would not have thought much of it until he heard laughter. It was very late for kids to be outside, especially in his city. He decided to investigate further.

As he approached the park, he could see the young couple inside the fenced area. The boy was no older than Jack, his skin stretched in a smile that reached his ears. He stood behind the swing-set, pushing the girl higher and higher. She was the one laughing as her pink hair blew across her face. She said something to the boy that made him slow the swing until it stopped. They kissed briefly and then walked away from the swing-set toward a parked motorcycle.

Jack jogged to meet them. They had already donned their helmets when he arrived. He snatched the keys from the boy's hand and mounted the motorcycle in a single movement, much to their protests. "Dude, get the hell off my bike!"

Before the boy could push him, Jack showed him the knife. The pink-haired girl screamed and pulled away her lover. The weapon was Jack's only defense against people who could overpower him, and thankfully it scared people most of the time. He had used it for the first time mere hours ago against Luke. His was the only blood that had ever touched the blade.

Jack drove away swiftly, the roar of the motorcycle drowning out his thoughts. It was a good thing that the streets were nearly empty, seeing as he had only driven a similar vehicle once. Crashing was a distinct possibility.

CHAPTER EIGHTEEN

The ride was pleasantly uneventful. He swerved onto a couple of sidewalks accidentally, but no one caught him, and he had not been delayed. Now almost directly faced with his death, Jack ran on nerves and adrenaline as a car ran on gasoline. He was not afraid. He did not even think about how he would save Alix. He would figure it out when he got there.

Jack parked the motorcycle far away from the warehouse so the noise would not announce his presence sooner than he wanted. He left the bike between a medical plaza and an apartment complex, propping it against the graffitied walls. Sunrise was no more than two hours away, judging by the lighter sky. He needed to get Alix out of the warehouse before then. She could hide in one of the abandoned fast-food restaurants nearby if he was too late, but he despised the idea of her being alone for the entire day.

He passed a trio of model bushes that were mounted on concrete poles at the street corner. The flat green things may have once been cheerful, but they were now ugly and tarnished by rain. At least they announced the name of the street.

His pace quickened as he approached the set of warehouses. They had been out of business for a long time. The doors and windows were all sealed shut with bricks and wooden panels. Old banners advertising acting and dancing schools fluttered in the breeze. Another sign told him that the warehouse had once guaranteed to beat any price in town.

"Good to know," he said under his breath. Gianna would not have told him to meet her and Luke here if there was no entrance, so he continued to search.

Jack walked down the sidewalk until he reached another bricked-up entrance. He stopped, for this one was different. A poster was taped onto the bricks, a poster that should not have been there.

"Space for rent," he read. This space could not be for rent. It was closed for eternity, until future occupants decided to destroy it. He examined it closer and saw that the poster was very old. When he touched it, it was wet and crumbly with rain and dirt. On the other hand, the tape was new. He prodded the middle of the poster and withdrew his hand shortly afterward. The surface underneath the words was hollow. His chest tightened in excitement and fear. The buzz in his head drowned out all previously existing thoughts.

Jack ripped off the poster in a single sweep, letting it fall to the ground. It rolled across the sidewalk, and he squatted down to meet a large hole in the wall. Bricks had been torn out to form a space wide enough for him to walk through. He licked his lips nervously and peered inside.

No one was there to meet him. Unfortunately, he did not carry a flashlight, and he could not see well in the darkness of the building. He could make out storage racks that reached the ceiling and held decaying pallets in place. Straight in front of him was a path that led all the way to the back of the building. If someone was hiding, he or she would be there.

Jack walked as fast as he could without making a sound. If he had learned anything in the past year, Luke and the Hunters were the types to announce their presence right off the bat. Something was different about this, since the warehouse was silent. Perhaps he had gotten the wrong address. Yes, that was it. Alix's life was in danger, and he had gone to the wrong building. He rolled his eyes.

It became more and more obvious as his thoughts cleared. The Hunters used Alix as bait once, and they were not finished. They waited with her for Jack to arrive, then they would kill the two Dusk Walkers at the same time. All he had to figure out was how to rescue her and get a ten-year-old girl past three trained killers, superpowers aside.

And they knew exactly where he was.

Because of the microchip, Jack was a beacon. If he went to Alix, Luke would kill him. If he ran, Gianna would find him, and then Luke would kill him. He wiped the cold sweat from his forehead. He drew his knife and continued to walk toward the back of the building with steps that grew louder by the second.

There were so many places to hide. The Hunters were

prepared, so they probably had night-vision goggles or something of the like. Their vision impairment meant nothing in this situation. They were at an advantage to him: The Dusk Walkers had not gained better night vision after the Explosion. They had only been rendered enemies of natural light. Cordy still had burns from several months ago, when she had forgotten to close the blinds during the day.

When he reached the far end of the warehouse, pyramids of moldy cardboard boxes, stacked as high as the ceiling, met him. Jack grimaced at the perfect labyrinth. It was a game of cat and mouse, and there were three cats. The cats knew where the mouse was at all times, and all the mouse wanted was to find his cheese. The mouse had to get to the cheese before the cats got to him, and that was not even the biggest challenge of them all.

As he rounded a pyramid of boxes, he caught a glimpse of movement. He leapt back behind the boxes, breathing carefully through his nose and listening for any noise. If it was a Hunter, he or she would find him soon, and he would have failed in his mission to find Alix. His jaw clenched painfully at the thought. He did not think highly of the Hunters, but he could not picture them killing a child as young as her. They would most likely drag her to some sort of experimental facility and put her through hell until she wished she were dead.

He made his decision. He could not allow either fate for his youngest friend. He left his hiding spot and found the source of the movement that he had spotted before.

"Jack!" His face split into a hysterical grin, and he

dropped to his knees in front of a large dog cage. Alix gripped the bars tightly. She did not appear hurt. They both began to speak at the same time.

"Be quiet, I'll get you out."

"You came! Are you insane?"

"Are you all right?"

"Jack…"

"I still can't believe you followed me to the hospital."

"Jack!"

"What?" He followed her gaze and looked over his shoulder. Three silhouettes approached from the darkness. The cats had found him. Fingers snapped, and the light above the cage crackled until it lit. It illuminated Alix's face, wet with fresh tears, and the faces of the Hunters. As he had suspected, they wore green nightvision goggles. Upon the arrival of the light, they removed their seeing aids. Gianna was the first to move.

"I can't watch this." She shook her head and retreated behind another pyramid of boxes.

Luke and Rae remained, both carrying their semiautomatics. Jack swallowed hard. That was it. He had failed Alix and had broken his promise to himself to save her. He turned away from the Hunters and looked to her once more, putting his hand on hers. Her skin was as warm as a low fire.

"I'm sorry," he whispered, now incapable of even forcing a smile. "You can turn your back if you want."

He stood slowly, protecting Alix as much as he could. Luke's pistol was raised. Jack's heart beat ferociously, and for a moment it could have exploded. He tried to look at Luke's eyes, but his gaze kept dropping to the gun. The gun that contained the bullet that would send him to the clouds…or to the fires—heaven or hell, if either existed. He was about to find out.

Jack saw Luke pull back the safety trigger. He might have seconds left before he died, if he was lucky. His knees trembled, and he hoped Alix had turned her back. There was nowhere to run. He was at the gallows, and the noose tightened around his neck. After he died, what would happen? Luke would shoot Alix? He would take her to a test lab? Jack could not let that happen. He could not die now. He couldn't die.

"Wait—"

Luke had already squeezed the trigger.

☢

"Is he dead?"

Luke took his time to answer. Rae's voice was emptier than usual, bringing him out of his trance. Time stood still in that moment, after Alix screamed and covered her hands with her face, and after Jack's head snapped backward so swiftly that it looked as though it would fly right off his neck.

Luke holstered his gun and knelt next to the body. He had just killed a child. Jack had only been two months short of turning eighteen, so he was still a minor. And Luke had shot him mercilessly in the head. His age hardly mattered, though. Putting Jack's death off by a couple of months would not have made a difference. "Luke?"

"Yeah. He's dead."

The boy's blue eyes were wide open. Luke tore his gaze away from the empty stare and placed his fingers over Jack's eyelids, closing them. He could be sleeping now, just as he had been when he was in the holding cell at the Hunters' precinct. Of course, he had been faking slumber then. Luke had always had trouble seeing the Dusk Walkers as real children. He had tried not to, because it made his job even trickier. Now he could only see the youth in Jack and Alix. Luke had already taken one life. He did not know how he would cope with taking several more.

He took the knife from Jack's belt. The weapon had harmed him earlier that night, but Luke did not care. Jack had used it in self-defense because he had not wanted to die, yet he had come to the warehouse to sacrifice himself for Alix. Seeing the situation that way hurt so much more.

Alix had retreated to the corner of the cage, her knees pulled up against her chest. Her eyes were red, but no tears fell. She stared at him with a fiery hatred. She was brave for a ten-year-old. Luke would have pictured her crying in fear and misery, but he could only see flames in her glare. His heart sank even lower when he remembered that Roy wanted him to kill Alix too. His captain was also convinced that the three other Dusk

Walkers and the brother-and-sister team would come for their friends, and he had instructed the Hunters to put them all down upon their entrance. It was going to be a slaughterhouse.

Luke would allow Alix some time with Jack to show her that he had compassion in his heart, which she probably did not believe. He moved Jack away from the door of the dog cage and drew the key to the padlock. Alix gripped the bars with white knuckles. He thought nothing of it until he touched the metal of the cage. Uttering a short gasp, he withdrew his hand. Her fire had burned the tips of his fingers.

"I'm going to let you out." He raised his hands in surrender.

"What are you gonna do after that?"

He said nothing. Instead, he tossed the key through the bars of the cage. "There. Let yourself out." She hesitated, then her tiny fingers snatched up the metal object.

"Luke." He whirled around. Gianna stood only yards away, staring at Jack's body with wide eyes. She did not need to see the dead Dusk Walker who had already brought him so much shame. He rushed to her side and led her behind a pyramid of boxes. "Did you kill him?"

Saying, "yes" like he had to Rae seemed wrong. He was more ashamed to say it to Gianna, for she was not as much of a rock as the younger Hunter. Gianna could read his face, and she had already seen the body. She was still weak from the concussion, but she was far from stupid.

"Wow…"

"What?" Luke sat on a stack of wooden pallets, the grief settling in him and tears coming to his eyes. "You didn't think I had it in me to kill?"

"No," admitted Gianna. She toyed with the frame of her glasses, a nervous tick of hers. "I was also thinking about when Roy told us to get rid of the Dusk Walkers. You didn't want to. What changed?"

Luke glanced in Jack's direction. Although he could not see the body, he knew it was still there. "I don't know, it just happened. If it helps, it'll probably be the thing that I'll regret the most in my life."

"I'm not mad, Luke. Or disappointed." She knelt in front of him and pushed his hair back from his face. "I just need to know that I can trust your actions. I need to know that you can take care of our baby when it's born."

"I can." That was a promise, not a fact. "But Roy's our captain. If he tells us to do something, we have to do it, right?"

"I'm not sure about Roy anymore. He may be our superior, but something's just not right about him. He should know that killing isn't an answer. I think something must have happened when he found out about the attack on his daughter. Especially since he lost his wife to radiation poisoning after the Explosion, I would expect him to be a little edgy, but this has gone too far."

Luke had forgotten about Roy's wife. Gianna had been the one to tell him about her not long after they met. Their captain never spoke of the tragedy, of course. His daughter was probably all he had left. Her attack had not been fatal, but it must have ruined Roy. It was possibly enough to drive him insane.

"Please, baby, do this for us. You're going to have a family soon. I don't want our child to find out that their dad killed the Dusk Walkers."

"It's too late now. Jack's dead, and I can't take that back. I could always go apologize, but something tells me he won't listen."

"Maybe so," said Gianna, so much calmer than him. She would be a good parent, unlike him. "Don't forget that there are still the four girls left. Also, the brother and sister that you and Rae mentioned are still alive. You can choose not to hurt them."

"Then what am I supposed to do with them?"

"I don't know. Arrest them all. Take them to the lab. Just don't kill them." She spoke as if the tasks were simple. The reason why the kill order was reasonable was to prevent the children from ever escaping their authority. It would be impossible to gather them all together, the fight being unbalanced in numbers and powers. If they all worked together, the six teenagers could beat the Hunters easily, unless Luke aimed to kill. He put his head in his hands.

"Guys," said Rae, suddenly at Gianna's side. "We're going to have company very soon."

"The Dusk Walkers?"

She nodded, her lips thin. "I heard them outside. Alix is with Jack. He's still dead."

Luke disliked the tone that she used, but decided not to comment. She would simply sneer at him, or they would argue. "What's the plan?"

"We stay here, we stay quiet, and we wait for Roy," said Gianna. "We have no equipment to overpower six superpowered kids."

"Roy?" said Rae. "You called him?"

"Yeah, he said that he would bring backup." Gianna looked to him. If they were lucky, Roy's backup would be able to take out the children without the Hunters lifting a hand. Voices approached the warehouse, finding the hole in the wall that Luke had left for Jack. He put a finger to his lips. He and Gianna did not budge, and Rae turned invisible.

"Alix! You okay?" said one voice. There was a short pause, and then some of the children gasped in horror as they recognized the body.

"He's dead!" A second voice, rather pointlessly.

"I'm going to kill those bastards if it's the last thing I do," said the unknown boy. Luke could only distinguish his voice from the others because of his deeper intonations. He could not tell if all six kids were present.

The grieving stopped abruptly, and Luke heard something different. Someone coughed and wheezed to get his breath back, as if he had been underwater for too long. There was no mistaking the person's identity.

He and Gianna shared a look. Relief and dread filled his mind. Now what were they supposed to do? They had nothing holding the six, now seven children in place while they awaited Roy's arrival. Jack was alive.

CHAPTER NINETEEN

Once Jack was able to breathe almost normally again, he looked around to see what all the turmoil was about. He did not know where he was or why he was short of air. First, he took in his surroundings: Cordy, Eva, Lily, Alix, Meg, and William all stared at him in shock.

"You're in rude health," said Meg with big blue eyes. He blinked rapidly, not understanding the expression. He saw that tears had recently fallen on each of the Dusk Walkers' pale cheeks.

"Why're you all crying?" His voice was hoarse. He propped himself up on his elbows and stared at the cardboard boxes and wooden pallets that were nearby. It was the inside of a warehouse. The sight of it all gave him a *déjà vu* feeling that was very recent. Memories of his lost years did not cause it. In fact, he could almost remember why he was there.

"Well," said Lily. She bit her lip. "You were dead."

Confused, he glanced to Eva, who quickly dried her face with her sleeve. She never cried, so he had probably been dead. Of course. He remembered now. The Hunters had brought Alix to this warehouse to lure him to his death, and then Luke had shot him. In fact, the boom of the gun still resounded in his mind, even though the wound in his forehead had healed.

"I'll be damned..." He grinned. He couldn't die! He was nearly invincible. "Whoa, wait a second. How'd you know that Alix and I were here?"

"Charles tracked you both down," said Cordy, gesturing ahead, where an invisible ghost likely was. She sat nearest to his head, and he could see the tear tracks on her face. Her eyes were streaked with red. "But we were too late."

"Hey..." He took her hand. "It's no big deal. I'm alive now." Jack sat up straight, and while doing so, he caught a glimpse of movement out of the corner of his eye. He whirled around. His killer stood ten paces away, followed by Gianna and Rae. Jack could not read his expression, nor those of his companions. The blond was cold and emotionless, as she usually appeared, but Luke and Gianna's faces were not as easy to interpret. They seemed unable to decide whether to express dread or relief, looking as if they felt both. Jack concluded that something had been knocked loose after the bullet to his brain, because that was impossible.

"You're not dead," said Luke.

"I got better." Jack swallowed hard. All of the people he cared about were next to him, in plain sight of the Hunters. They could easily hurt his friends, or even kill them. The only exit to the warehouse was at the far end of the building, past his enemies. If they were lucky, the seven children had a chance of escaping as long as they fought hard enough.

He thought he was hallucinating when Luke lifted Jack's knife into the air, holding it by the blade. "This is yours." He slid it across the floor toward the weapon's owner, who picked it up and secured it in his belt.

Jack immediately returned his gaze to Luke, who was not to be trusted. That was when he noticed the bandage around his forearm, partially hidden by the sleeve of his jacket. "How's the arm?"

"Horrible, thanks to you." Luke pushed the sleeve down. "And it turns out that I just barely missed you at the hospital earlier. It was the same building. I must've left right before you walked in. You went to see your dad…that was unexpected, to say the least."

"Well, you know what they say," said Jack, beginning to stand up. Since his adversary did not react, everyone else was on his or her feet by the time that he finished his sentence. "Always expect the unexpected."

Several of the girls shrieked. Jack stumbled backward, nearly tripping over Eva's foot.

"What the hell?" said William. They all gaped at the source of the explosion that had blasted through the panels barricading one of the windows. It had ripped apart a chunk of the bricked wall as wide as the length of a large car.

Jack looked to Luke. "Was that one of yours?"

The Hunters bore the same shocked look as Jack.

Gianna shook her head. "That was a grenade. A small bomb, or something of the like. It wasn't manufactured in a factory, I can tell you that. And there's something else..." She stared into the distance, eyes squinted in concentration. Her expression shifted in less than a second, her jaw dropping and her brows raising. "No, duck!"

Jack dived, bringing Eva down with him. They fell against the empty dog cage with a crash, and his head hit the floor roughly, but his arm had cushioned hers. He was unable to breathe properly. The tightness in his throat burned, and then it was as cold as ice. He was numb for a moment, no longer than two brief seconds. As soon as he felt the overwhelming pain in his neck return, he could also feel the hot scarlet blood that streamed onto his shirt and sweater. A bullet had passed through the side of his neck, away from anything major. If it had hit him an inch or two to the left, he would have died. Again.

Eva was not as lucky as him. Blood, not his own, bloomed across her abdomen. He leaned closer and pulled her onto her back. He could not tell if any major organs had been touched, but she was still breathing, although with difficulty.

"Jack!" said Cordy. She and the others retreated behind a pyramid of cardboard boxes that were located off to the side of the building. Luke had vanished suspiciously, and Gianna and Rae hid behind the storage racks where they had emerged from earlier. The sniper was not theirs.

"Go, we'll be fine!" he tried to shout, but he choked

before he could finish, blood creeping into his throat. She seemed to understand and joined their friends.

"I tried to move out of the way…" said Eva. "Too slow." Jack scooped her up, adrenaline helping him all the way. It was too risky to hide with Cordy because it would involve running directly into the sniper's line of fire. His only choice was to join Gianna and Rae. They were the closest, so he ran. He completely ignored the two Hunters when he arrived, setting Eva down on a wooden pallet. He was panting now, perspiration beading on his forehead. So that he would not die of blood loss before he could do anything else for her, he covered his wound with his right hand, putting pressure on it.

Gianna arrived at his side. "Is she okay?"

"What do you think?"

"That sniper isn't supposed to be there. Luke's gone to call him off. It's too far for me to disable it from here."

Jack did not care. He could only look at Eva, who struggled to breathe. She stared at the wound below her ribs, curling her lips in disgust. He knew nothing of first aid and felt more helpless than he ever had. He was exhausted beyond belief and could not think straight. He could only sit on the platform, holding her warm body against his.

"Wait a second," said Rae slowly. She was talking to Gianna, so he did not turn around. He listened, the majority of his attention on Eva. Not knowing where to put his hand that did not cover his wound, he gripped hers tightly. They had held hands before, but with the added drama of her possible death, this was so different. "You said that you called Roy for backup. Maybe that sniper was it."

"Crap," said Gianna. "I had hoped that he would bring a couple of cops to arrest the kids. Not, you know, kill them."

"We're not dead yet," said Jack. Eva did not meet his eyes, and he feared that she would leave him, in his arms like his father had. With any luck, Cordy would be able to summon her ghost if it came to that. He gave himself a mental kick. It would not come to that.

"I can see that. I just meant that Roy and the sniper had *intended* to kill you."

"Just piss off, okay? Go back to your boyfriend, I doubt you're a target."

The two women glanced at each other, then left him alone. Looking down at Eva, Jack realized that he had never seen her in pain before. When he felt the familiar prickling of his skin healing over his own injury, he moved his hand onto her injury in an attempt to slow her bleeding. When he saw that it was the same hand that he had just bled all over, he pulled it away. Eva stopped him, placing her hand on top of his. "Lucky…you got to come back after you died."

Jack shook his head. He bit the inside of his cheek so he would not cry. "Shut up, I love you." Slowly, very slowly, he came to grasp what he had just said. The words had escaped his mouth like a breath held for too long. A short puff of air escaped his lungs. She finally knew. It was no longer a secret he kept, which brought him great relief. He only had to worry about her reaction.

Eva's eyelashes fluttered in an act of surprise. He could not tell if that was a good or a bad thing. Her fingers wriggled beneath his, and he loosened his grip, dreading the worst. Then Eva grabbed his shirt collar and pulled him closer to her and kissed him on his lips. It was as if someone had socked him in the stomach. She was kissing him! Her eyelids slammed shut against his cheek. Their mouths pressed together clumsily, and her fingers grasped his shirt in an iron grip. This was one of the things that he had dreamt about for almost three years. For a moment, nothing else mattered in the world.

They pulled apart after what felt like hours, and then seconds. Eva breathed more deeply now. She took her hand off of her wound and gasped quietly. Through the hole the bullet had torn in her shirt, they saw that the previously severe bullet wound in her abdomen was now just a scar on the mend.

"Oh my God," she said, sitting up as if everything was all right. "Your neck."

Jack's hand flew to his throat and felt nothing out of the ordinary. "What about it?"

"Your blood." Eva stared at him in amazement, but he still did not understand. She reached up, and her fingers brushed the spot on his neck where his own wound had healed and the blood had dried. Her touch tickled his skin, but he doubted that was the point. As soon as he forced himself to think, he understood the same thing that she had. When he had been shot, he had bled onto his hand. Then he had put the same hand on Eva's wound. She had healed after his blood had come into contact with hers.

"Whoa."

She let out a bark of laughter. "Understatement."

They climbed to their feet. Jack had not heard the sniper fire his rifle since the two of them had been hit. He did not believe that Luke had succeeded in calling off the shooting. The man hardly had any authority to do such a thing. Jack then asked himself why the Hunters were defending the Dusk Walkers in the first place. That night, nothing made any sense to him.

Jack and Eva stepped out of their hiding place, staying out of the sniper's line of fire while moving into eyeshot of their friends.

"Eva, are you okay?" said Lily from across the space, clearly gaping at the blood on her shirt.

"I'm fine," said Eva.

"But you were shot!"

Jack took over. "It turns out that not only can't I die, my blood can heal people." He could not help but laugh at the two new discoveries. His power was not quite as useless as he had believed.

"You're joking," said Meg. He shook his head, for it was all true. "What next, you're going to start growing extra limbs?"

As he frowned in puzzlement at the possibility, Luke ran past him, only a blur to his eyes. The Hunter slowed to a stop in front of his two partners. Jack pretended not to listen.

"Roy's the sniper. He tried to shoot me when I got there! But he's the only one I saw. I'm guessing he got the grenade from the lab."

"You're all right, aren't you?" said Gianna.

"Yeah. You were right about Roy, though. He's officially bad news," said Luke. Jack looked their way with raised eyebrows. The Hunters' boss wanted to kill them. That put Jack and Luke on the same side. "More importantly, we're targets now. We've got to get out of here. Conveniently, the only way out is the hole in the wall facing Roy."

Luke turned on the spot, hands on his hips. He glanced around the back of the warehouse, as though an exit would suddenly appear in the wall. While he came to the end of his circular search, his eyes met Jack's. Taking the risk, Jack made a small nod for Luke to join him and Eva. Now that all ten of the people present were targets, they could easily work together to make a plan to get out safely.

"Wait here," said Luke to Gianna and Rae. He walked up to the Dusk Walkers, only glancing once toward Eva before returning to Jack. "I take it you heard me."

"Yeah. Sucks about your boss. You can't trust anyone these days, huh?"

"Don't push it, kid." Luke glared at him. Jack made no reaction until he saw the man glance upward slightly. Knowing that the blood on his forehead stood out like a lightning-bolt scar, Jack combed his hair over his forehead to hide some of the vanished wound. Luke cleared his throat. "Do you have a plan to get out of here, by any chance?"

Jack looked at Eva, who scrunched up her face in consideration for a moment. She shook her head. "Nope."

"Thanks a lot for the help."

"No problem," said Jack coolly. "Anything to help the guy who killed me."

"Don't start—"

"Wait a second," said Eva. She smiled, and her face seemed to glow, but Jack doubted that Luke noticed the glowing part. "We could burn down the building. Alix could set it on fire, then the Hunters could tell everybody that we died here. No one has to know anything else."

He stared at her, his jaw dropped in amazement. The plan was perfect. A genuine smile returned to his face. Not only could they escape the warehouse unscathed, but the government would no longer hunt them. If the Hunters were up to giving the Dusk Walker a hand for once.

"That's all great," said Luke in a voice that was too bitter for Jack's taste. "For you guys. That doesn't help Gianna, Rae or me."

"Refresh my memory: Why do we want to help you?" said Jack.

"Because we can help you."

"Why would you want to help us?"

Luke almost looked ashamed. With a short hesitation, he answered, "Now that Roy wants to kill us, you're all we've got. And we're all you've got."

"Then we're doomed."

He rolled his eyes. "I'm serious. You could all die."

"Well, we wouldn't want that, would we? Fifteen minutes ago you were completely comfortable with blowing me away," said Jack.

Luke's expression did not waver for a few moments, and then the next thing that Jack knew, he had been shoved out of their hiding place, directly into the sniper's line of fire. After he regained his balance, he noticed a tiny red dot on his chest. With a yell, he dropped flat to the ground as a bullet hit the wall behind him. Jack scrambled as quickly as he could behind the storage racks, glaring at Luke.

"You pushed me," he accused weakly.

"I could easily do that to all of you right now, one by one. I'm more than fast enough. But I haven't, and I won't. So just this once, will you help us out? We can come up with something together that will get us all out of here alive."

"Why don't we ask the others if they have any ideas?" said Eva. She motioned across the wall toward the place where Cordy, Lily, Alix, Meg, and William were crouched. "We'll have to get there first. Rae is invisible, so she can just walk ahead without Roy seeing her. The rest of us can run across in pairs. I don't think your captain is a trained sniper."

"He isn't," said Luke. "That's why he missed you. Before he was a cop, he was into the sciences, but that's all I know. He isn't exactly a big talker."

"Then we should be able to get there easily," said Eva. Jack looked at the length they would have to cross. The space was the width of a small house, more than enough space for Roy to shoot them. They would have to be quick.

Rae stepped forward. "I'll go first, then." She vanished, and Jack could only listen for the tapping of her shoes against the floor to know where she was. She walked at a steady pace until she reached the other side of the empty space. On the wall, the red dot of Roy's gun did not waver.

Luke and Gianna went next, running as fast as her legs would carry her, while he shielded her from Roy. Jack's senses were keen in that moment, and he heard the bullet fire. He sucked in a gasp between his teeth, the length they ran suddenly seeming so much longer. The bullet hit the wall, and Luke and Gianna arrived safely.

"By now he knows you and I are coming," said Eva. Her features were hard and pensive. "He'll fire more than once. Would you mind standing on my left? To, you know…"

"Protect you?" said Jack without repressing an eager grin. "Always."

She snorted and rolled her eyes. As she crouched in preparation to run, he did the same and took a deep breath. Nothing would stop Roy from unleashing a hail of bullets that they could not escape. He could only hope that the man was inexperienced enough with his weapon to not do so. "On three. One, two, three…go!"

They pushed off and ran. Eva was a step faster than him, and he sprinted to catch up to her pace. They had not reached the dog cage when she saw the red dot appear in front of them. Roy had predicted their path and fired before they even reached the target area.

Eva threw out her arm and Jack doubled over just in time. His heartbeat deafened him as he felt the bullet fly through his hair. It had missed by less than an inch. He cursed as he straightened, and they raced to the finish line. He truly felt as though he had just run a marathon, despite it having only been a few yards.

Jack was short of breath when they arrived in front of their companions, but Eva was completely calm due to her endurance. He saw that Luke was the same, the crossing having been no more than a quick walk for him. His arm was around Gianna's waist, whose glasses were askew. Rae was visible once more, and she stood apart from everyone else. Alix and Lily sat on the ground, elbows on their knees. Meg and William leaned against the wall side by side, and Cordy smiled when he looked her way.

"Are you sure that there's only one sniper?" said Jack to Luke and Gianna. They nodded. Luke had witnessed Roy's intentions, and Gianna could sense the technology around them. Unfortunately, she was not strong enough to disable the rifle. "Then why don't we go out that way?" Jack pointed to the wall that was opposite Roy and the exit.

"There's no door," said Luke.

Jack scowled at him, using all the will he could muster to not comment. He was perfectly aware of the lack of door. "We could blast a hole through the wall." He looked at Alix when he spoke.

"You want me to throw a fireball through the wall?" She raised her eyebrows in doubt.

"Yeah. What's wrong with that?"

"Nothing, it's just that…I've never done anything like that before. What if I can't do it?" Now that nine pairs of eyes were turned her way, she bowed her head in shame, and her cheeks flushed.

He squatted down next to her. "Are you kidding me? You always make sure that we don't freeze in the winter, you had the guts to follow me to the hospital, and you stood up to the Hunters when they brought you here. There's absolutely nothing you can't do after all that! Now why don't you come save all of our butts? You're the only one who can."

"You're just saying that to cheer me up," she mumbled, her chin against her chest.

"I'm not," said Jack. That made Alix raise her head and smile.

"Hey," said a voice that made Jack turn around. Luke stood behind him, holding two bright-red containers. "I found these. There's a ton of them just across the street. I was fast enough to get them before Roy noticed."

"Gasoline?" guessed Jack.

"Very good."

"I don't think Al needs that to blast a hole through the wall." He looked at Alix for her opinion, and she shook her head, confirming his assumption.

"No, but she needs it to light the place on fire." When no one commented, Luke continued. "While you guys work on blasting said hole through the wall, I'll line the place in gasoline. Once we're safe, we'll light a fire, distracting Roy, then we'll go our separate ways. I'll tell the press that the Dusk Walkers died in the fire, and it'll all be over."

"What about you? Roy's your boss, and he wants to kill you. How's that gonna work? It's not like you could just go back to the office."

"We'll change our names and go into hiding if we have to. Without our help, he's powerless against both you and me," was his reply. "He can't steal a sniper rifle every time he sees us, if he ever does again."

Jack still disliked working with his enemies, although so far it was not as horrible as he would have imagined.

He cursed himself at the thought, but he knew it was true. If Luke had wanted to harm them, he would have done it already. "Fine. Let's light this baby up."

CHAPTER TWENTY

While Luke collected containers of gasoline, zipping back and forth from across the street to the back of the warehouse, Eva conducted the operation. She shouted and gestured for everyone in the group to do their assigned parts, making sure they were outside Roy's line of fire. Jack had very little to do, his job mostly consisting of telling an invisible Rae to tell Luke to begin pouring the gasoline.

Cordy, with Charles's help, served as a satellite dish over the area. They perceived any arrivals in the area, and the ghost diverted their path by pushing street signs into the middle of the roads. Gianna and Lily helped Alix manage the hole in the wall. Meg sat against a box propped against the wall, fingers glued to her temples. Her eyes were shut in concentration as she kept tabs on Roy's thoughts. William guided light particles around the warehouse to help Luke see where he placed the gasoline.

"Done." Luke slowed to a jog, an empty container of gasoline in his hands. Jack spotted half a dozen more red plastic parts scattered around the warehouse. "How's the wall coming along?"

"Nearly done," said Alix. She sat cross-legged on the

floor and took a deep breath. Her chest rose and fell several times before she rubbed her thumbs and index fingers together. Two small flames sparked in her hands, and she pulled them apart until there was a distance of a foot between her palms. The fire united into an orb, no bigger than a tennis ball at first, then expanding into the size of a beach ball.

When it was the right diameter, Alix finally sent it forward with a swift snap of her fingers. It crashed through the wall like butter, shaping a hole big enough for even Luke to walk through. Those in the immediate area, which included Jack, Eva, Luke, Rae, and William, were all covered in a thin layer of dust. Alix received the most of it. Her eyelashes and eyebrows were whitened, giving her a permanently surprised look.

"Piece of cake." She smiled, the gap between her two front teeth a charming addition to the powder on her face.

One by one, the Dusk Walkers, the Hunters, and the twins all climbed through the opening, exiting the building at last. Jack stepped outside and saw the pink and yellow of the sunrise in the sky. They would have to find somewhere to hide within the hour or the sun would burn them to a crisp. He considered their established locations and came to the conclusion that their nearest hideout was location four, the house in District Three where his friends were meant to retreat after his departure for the hospital.

"Hey, watch this." Alix tugged on his sleeve. She motioned for everyone else to step back from the building, and she leaned down. When she blew swiftly onto the line of gasoline, a spark carried an enormous flame inside of the building, spreading like wildfire. Many of the cardboard towers burned instantly, the tips of the fire tickling the high ceiling.

The heat was so immense that Jack could feel it on his face. "That is something else, Al. We'll have to be extra careful around you now."

She skipped into his welcoming arms, leaping to clasp her fingers together behind his neck. He stumbled backward with the weight of the child, laughing as he did so. Her glee was contagious. She had not been this happy in months. Alix was always eager to help out, and she was rarely allowed to prove her worth. Now she had finally gotten her chance.

"Roy's split the area," said Meg. "He's gone now."

"We're gonna go," said Luke after Jack placed Alix back on her feet. "You should leave too. The sun's coming up."

He nodded, his smile melting away as the three adults turned to leave. The situation was all too perfect. The Dusk Walkers had escaped death while at the same time becoming legally dead, the Hunters would leave them alone, they had new allies in the twins, and Eva had kissed him. There was a downside; he knew it.

Roy. The man would still hunt the gifted folk down. Luke had mentioned that Roy had almost no forces to rely upon, but Jack was certain that he would find a method to get his way, sooner or later.

Cordy tapped his shoulder and made a quick nod that meant they were leaving. They would get a quick ride from Meg and William back to location four. When he learned of their transportation, he asked himself how all seven of them would fit in a car with only five seats. He was about to find out.

On their way to the warehouse, five teens were able to fit into the Camry. Now that Alix and Jack were there, their solution was to have him sit on the floor in between the front and backseats. Lily morphed into a small cat and curled up on Alix's lap.

He sat with his back against the right-side door, playing with the person's shoelaces who sat in the seat above him. When he tried to meet Eva's eyes, she only pulled her feet away from him, and onto the seat. Jack tried desperately to understand why she would kiss him one moment and then pull away from him the next. He had done nothing wrong.

Horror clocked him in the face when he considered the possibility that Eva had not kissed him because she reciprocated his feelings. She might have cursed him with a fake first kiss. No, she was not that cruel. She would never do that to him, but he could not stop himself from developing the details of the idea.

It made sense. They had believed that Eva would die. Jack had told her that he loved her, and she had pitied him. It could hardly even be thought of as respect. If her feelings were false, she had hurt him even more than if she had died.

He risked a glance in her direction. Streetlights

flickered against her face, yellow and then white and then black in no particular order. She still kept a careful eye on her shoes, her shoulders tense. He knew from living with four girls that the position meant something. Eva knew that he stared at her, but she did not want to return the favor.

He could not hate her, not even for a second. If she asked him to jump off a cliff, he would obey. Any wish of hers was his command. It had been that way for years, and its end was not anywhere in sight.

Jack was freed from his cramped position when they arrived at the house. On the outside, it was very old, built at least a hundred years ago. Faded orange bricks constituted the walls, and rotted flowerbeds sat under boarded-up windows. The front door, unlike the other entrances, was not permanently closed. Red bars locked the doorway, but the Dusk Walkers knew how to get inside. They also had an emergency exit. One of the windows on the second floor was not completely secured by the wooden boards. It could be pushed open if that was one's intent, and a person could jump from the frame onto the hard ground.

He opened his door and climbed out of the car. His joints cracked as he stretched his legs, arms, and back. His friends exited the vehicle one by one, tossing their backpacks over their shoulders. He reminded himself that he would require another, as well as supplies to put inside. The twins stayed put.

"Bye, guys," said William from the driver's window. He and Lily exchanged a wave.

"Until next time," she said, sounding shyer than he had ever heard. The Dusk Walkers began to walk toward the barbed wire that fenced off the building.

"Oi!" called Meg. Jack turned around and walked back to the car. "You've got our numbers, right?"

Jack nodded, thinking of the slip of paper in the back pocket of his jeans. "By the way, what's with the British slang? You've got a Brooklyn accent."

"Ever heard of Withencroft Industries?" said Meg, not appearing to have noticed his question. The company name rang a bell. He had come across it while listening to the news. "My dad is Callum Withencroft, owner and creator of the only corporation that is holding this city together. He's completely off his rocker, but who isn't nowadays?"

Jack shrugged. Meg and William's father was a rich businessman, and their mother had died after the experiment on the twins. "What does this have to do with—"

"That makes us practically royalty. Since I was little, I've always thought that that wasn't enough. I'm horrible with accents, but I've made it a hobby of mine to pick up slang from across the pond. It makes me feel like a real princess."

It both amused him and distressed him that the twins were so high in the city's hierarchy. It was comical, seeing as he was part of the lowest section of the pyramid. On the other hand, the twins put him and his friends at a greater risk that he had initially imagined. If anyone found out about the Dusk Walkers' continued existence, they were all done for. However, Meg and William had gone fifteen years without anyone knowing about their powers, so he knew that they could keep a secret.

"We'd better get back home," said William. "We've got school in an hour."

Jack raised a brow. "After everything you've done tonight, you're going to school?"

"I've got a French test at second period!"

"Can't you skip it?"

William's jaw dropped as though it was the most appalling thing imaginable. "No! It's the most important test of that class for this term! If I flunk it, my dad'll eat my head for dinner!" Whether he was kidding or not was a mystery.

Meg unbuckled her seatbelt and leaned across her brother. She pushed a button on the door, and the window began to roll back down. "Cheerio!"

Jack waved as they drove down the street, telling himself that he would try to keep in touch with the twins after all. If it were not for them, the past night would have been completely different. They had helped him escape from the police station, they had given him a ride home, and they had come to his death. He had only met them hours ago.

There were no streetlamps, but the pink hue of the sky was clear enough to see his friends' expressions. Cordy and Lily smiled at him, eyes squinted with fatigue. Alix beamed brighter than ever, and Eva still avoided his gaze. Nobody spoke.

He mulled over the events of the past day and a half. Hopefully they would be able to take a break from all of the action of the past few days for as long as they could. If they stayed true to their word, the Hunters would not bother them anymore. The Withencroft twins had gone back to living their life. If Jack was lucky, things had returned to the way they had been before, maybe even better now. The Dusk Walkers would soon be legally dead, and no one would be on the hunt for them.

"All right, so who's keeping watch first?" said Lily, breaking the silence.

"I'll do it," said Cordy with a yawn. "Let's get some rest, guys."

They approached the first fence that blocked off the building. The barrier stood over six feet high, the top curled with barbed wire. A small passageway was off to the side, padlocked so that no one could enter. Eva kicked it down, and the door flew off its hinges and into the brown grass behind. The five teenagers hurried into the decaying yard and leaned the fence against the frame so that it would appear undamaged.

Another fence was in their way, this time much smaller. Without the barbed wire, they could climb over it easily. Jack helped Alix lift her short legs over the hurdle before he clambered over it inelegantly. The final obstacle in their way was a series of dirty red bars that blocked what was once the door to the old house. Cordy, Eva, and Alix worked to figure out how to get past it while Lily followed Jack to one of the wooden boards that blocked the windows.

A massive grey bear stared back at them with white eyes. Jack tilted his head at the strange graffiti and marched toward it. Plastic bags and empty soda cans crackled under his feet, the results of a challenge amongst local kids to see who could throw their trash the farthest. He peered at the bear carefully. The paint had to be decades old, yet it was still intact.

"It's only slightly unsettling," said Jack to Lily. She shook her head.

"In some cultures, the bear symbolizes resurrection or peace. Like tonight."

"What about the eyes?"

"Eyes represent premonition, and white eyes mean death," said Lily with a frown. "That is unsettling."

He snorted and ruffled her frizzy hair. "It's just graffiti. But it's funny that it hasn't been painted over. It's gotta be at least twenty years old…"

"We're in!" Cordy and Eva lifted the bars off their hinges, the tips of the metal burnt to black. The Dusk Walkers rushed inside, and Alix welded the rods together loosely. Due to the dull light that already shone through the bars, the teenagers would have to retreat to the second floor in order to avoid the sun.

"Cordy, you and him can look around upstairs," said

Eva. Jack jutted out his jaw as he realized that he was "him." She was ignoring him to the point where she could not even address him by name. "Make sure there are no squatters. This place is ours."

He followed Cordy up the rotting stairs. They arrived on the second floor of the house, discovering once-beautiful walls and floors that were now ruined by lack of use. She pushed open the doors on their right, peering inside in search for street rats like themselves. He did the same on the left and only found graffiti and dust bunnies wherever he looked. "It's clear!"

Eva, Lily, and Alix hurried up the stairs. "Nothing downstairs. It doesn't look like anyone's been here in ages."

"I call the mattress!" Alix ran into the old master bedroom, Lily running after her in her puppy form. Eva followed them, reminding them to lay down their sleeping pads in case of bugs.

There was a room with a broken chandelier and a vintage couch that had seen better days. Jack perched himself on the edge of the sofa, and Cordy watched him from the doorway. "I guess I'll get a couple of hours of shuteye, huh? I'm exhausted."

"I bet," she said. "But you might want to wash that blood off of you first."

"Oh, right." His hair had crusted to his forehead, and more blood had dried on his neck and hands. At the warehouse it had been unpleasant, but now it was hardly noticeable. All the same, he stood to walk to the old bathroom. He had seen a mirror earlier.

"Jack," said Cordy. She zipped open her backpack. "There's no running water."

He caught the water bottle and washcloth that she threw at him. "Thanks."

The door to the bathroom would not close all the way, nor would the lights turn on. He felt where the dried blood stretched his skin, so he would probably be able to remove most of it in the dark. Jack opened the water bottle and poured some of the liquid onto the washcloth. He had to scrub his face hard to get all of the blood off, and he would be pink by the end of the process.

While he wiped down the arch of his neck and shoulder, he could almost feel Eva's cool fingers touching him there like she had in the warehouse after their kiss. He wanted more than ever for her to talk to him. He was too afraid to approach her on his own.

He decided that it would still be acceptable to have some specks of blood on his skin, and he returned to the couch. Cordy had laid out her sleeping pad on top of the sofa for him. He opened his mouth to thank her for the favor, but she spoke before him. "Whatcha gonna do about Eva?"

Jack's jaw hung open in disbelief. "How…how does everyone know what I'm thinking about?"

"Well, it's obvious! The way you look at her and talk to her…don't think we haven't noticed. Also, she told me what happened in the warehouse."

He gave a miserable groan and fell onto the couch. "Damn the opposite gender."

"I'm going to pretend I didn't hear that," said Cordy. "Here's my advice: talk to her."

"But she's ignoring me! That means she doesn't want me to talk to her."

She threw back her head and guffawed. "Of course she wants you to talk to her, you naive idiot!"

"Screw you," said Jack. "If she wants me to talk to her, why is she ignoring me?"

The rolling of her eyes that followed indicated that he knew nothing about women. "Because…she kissed you on impulse, but she's not sure if you like her back! You've got to let her know that you do like her."

"But I did."

"I guess you weren't convincing enough. She thinks you could have said that to make her feel better. She was dying, after all."

Jack frowned at the chandelier. "How do I convince her?"

Cordy scoffed. "If I told you what to do, it wouldn't be right. It has to be personal." When he chewed his lip in thought, she stood to leave the room. "I'll let you sleep on it."

Still thinking, he turned onto his side and closed his

eyes. He had intended to think of a solution to his problem before he fell asleep, but he was unconscious as soon as his head hit the foam mattress, exhausted from the past day and a half.

CHAPTER TWENTY ONE

Luke had never guessed how difficult his next job would be. He had sent Gianna and Rae home while he stayed at the precinct. Roy was nowhere to be found, and his daughter Vanessa had disappeared from the hospital. A separate investigation led by a different department was underway, with no luck. Luke had met with the chief of police, who believed the story in which the Dusk Walkers perished in a fire. The chief had been told of Roy's betrayal and planned to reappoint the Hunters while they awaited news from the investigation. Since their job was finished, they could do nothing else.

Luke had agreed with the chief's recommendation to stay at the NYPD. The Hunters had a reputation to uphold, and he could not imagine retiring before he was thirty. Luke needed to work, so he worked.

He picked up his desk phone for the fourth time that afternoon, searching through online and paper directories to figure out which precincts to contact. He had made calls to various police stations across the country in order to get in touch with the Dusk Walkers' parents.

Most of them had moved away in order to cope with their distress or had accompanied the wave of the fearful who had fled the city because of the radiation's damage. The local authorities visited the mothers and fathers of the supposedly deceased teens to announce the death of their children. He had already contacted the precincts that would reach the families of Eva, Lily, and Alix. The grieving parents would surely call him back in rage or completely ignore his existence. He would not blame them.

Jack had no next of kin. Any relation of his that Luke could find was too distant. Therefore, Luke only had one family left to see. This would be the most difficult, since Cordy's parents lived in the city. He would have to visit them himself.

Luke went to the bathroom and splashed his face with water. It was far from cool enough to freshen his mood, but he twisted the metal knob until the water stopped running, and he wrenched a brown paper towel from the dispenser to dry his skin. He balled it up in his fist until his knuckles turned white. What had he gotten himself into? He could have killed the Dusk Walkers and the twins, arrested Jack, and move on with his life. He would have no secrets to hide. On the other hand, he would have killed six children and sentenced another to an eternity of confinement.

In the warehouse he had been satisfied with his decision regarding the impossible choice. No longer was this the case. Now he had to lie to parents about the deaths of their children, whom they had certainly loved. They had promised once that they would not interfere with the Hunters' responsibilities, and they had listened. In return, he was forced to tell them that he had indirectly killed the four teenagers. He wished that he could tell Cordy's parents the truth, as he had fought the urge to do so during every previous call to precincts. The unknowing officers across the country would have to carry out his dirty work and spread his lies. Nausea clenched his stomach.

"You all right, Detective?"

Luke straightened and glanced at the mirror. Sergeant Wagner entered the bathroom. The fair-haired man was a pain in the ass. If someone told Luke that the sergeant was merely a teenage boy in disguise, he would believe that person wholeheartedly. "Fine."

"Doncha have calls to make?"

"I'm taking a break." Luke unclenched his fist and tossed the paper towel into the garbage. "In fact, I should be getting back to them."

"I hear your girl's got a bun in the oven. Post-Explosion, salaries for cops have gone downhill. Anyway, most of what you do is considered volunteer work when it comes to payday. You've got minimal training, and you've only ever arrested one of your targets. And he escaped! And then you killed him! I mean, only a rogue cop would ever kill five kids—"

Sergeant Wagner's head cracked against the tile wall when he was sent flying backward. The bolt of electricity had hit him directly in his chest, lifting him off his feet.

"I can't go rogue," said Luke to Wagner's stirring body before he turned on his heels and left, regretting nothing.

"I'm not a cop."

Luke grabbed his jacket from the back of his chair and ripped the note with the addresses of Cordy's parents from his notepad. The stationary fell off his desk with a fluttering thump, and he leaned down to retrieve it. Before putting it back in its place, he hesitated and stared at the blank lines for a moment.

He reached into the top drawer of his desk and pulled out a black pen. He had made his choice the night before. He lied to everyone but Gianna and Rae about something that constituted a federal crime, and he did not care. If he was caught because of it, so be it.

Luke rapped on the door of apartment 624. This was his first time directly announcing a death, and he had been told it was brutal. He would be a part of the worst day of this woman's life, but he would have to get the lie over with.

The door swung open to reveal a woman thirty years his senior. Her graying hair frizzed in all directions, but she was smiling. "Hi, Marin." He tried to pull off an expression that was pleasant, but not pleased, and grim, but not gloomy.

He did not have to worry about his mood any longer. As soon as she recognized him, her smile fell faster than it took him to say hello.

"Detective," she said. Luke awaited a longer response, and a toddler crawled to the door, wrapping its arms around Marin's leg. She gave a tired sigh. She picked up the child. Her lips had grown so thin that they had been reduced to two strips of white between her nose and her chin. "Come inside. Excuse the mess, I'm taking care of my grandson for the weekend."

Luke closed the door behind him and followed Marin to the living room. He slowed in front of a low-standing bookshelf. Framed pictures sat atop it, mostly of two young women, one blonde and one brunette. He lifted one from the back. In the photo, on a red-and-white checkered blanket, he saw Marin and the two young women, the daughters still teenagers in the captured moment. Richard Lear was also there, his bald head shining in the sunlight of the picnic. Another member of the family sat in the front of the picture, wearing a pink T-shirt and her hair in a ponytail. Her hands were clasped in front of her knees, and she smiled without showing her teeth. He was glad that he had not hurt Cordy. The sight of the picture would have been so much worse if he had.

"What happened to her?" said Marin. She had watched him pick up the frame. The toddler was still in her arms, worn out from a long day of play.

"Maybe we should sit down—"

"No, tell me now. I'll tell her sisters when they get home, and I'll even call Richard if that would help." She would not look at him. Her voice was steady, but her lips trembled visibly. Her shoulders shook, and the toddler twisted around in confusion.

Luke took a deep breath and told himself that it was several times harder for Marin than it was for him. He knew that Cordy was alive. The girl's mother had lost her daughter years ago with no right to see her, all the while knowing that she resided in the same city. Marin had been forced to see pictures of her criminal daughter on television every week. She had most likely received floods of hate messages for having given birth to one of the Dusk Walkers. Luke licked his lips and got to the point. He followed his instructions: He had to be blunt.

"There was a fire last night. You might have seen it on the morning news, but we're trying to keep it covered up until things are figured out. Anyway, the Dusk Walkers all died inside the building. Whether it was by suffocation, burns, or what have you, we don't know yet. But Cordelia is dead. I'm very sorry."

Marin placed the puzzled toddler on the ground and pressed her hand to her chest, her fingers spread out in a fan. She turned her back, and he knew that she wanted to hide her tears. Luke placed the picture of the Lear family back onto the bookshelf, and he felt something touch his leg. He looked down and saw Marin's grandson, Cordy's nephew, patting his jeans with clumsy fingers. He gave the child a little push, leading him toward his grandmother. "Come on, let's go see Marin."

Mrs. Reid sat on the couch now, dabbing at her cheeks with a tissue paper. Luke sat across from her in the armchair and leaned forward, putting his elbows on his knees. "Do you need Richard and me to identify the body?"

"Well, we haven't exactly…found them yet." It was one of the factors of the fire that would cause people to be suspicious. Investigators would never find bodies, despite his confirmation that there should be five. He could only hope that his word was enough to convince the city that the Dusk Walkers were gone.

"How can you be sure that she's gone if you haven't found the body?"

"There was only one exit. And I was covering it."

The little boy stood between the stranger and his grandmother, glancing back and forth between the two. He knew by now that something was wrong.

"Nana?" he said to Marin, his face twisted in worry. "Why're you crying?"

She shook her head, and more curly hair popped loose. "It's nothing, Brandon. Go try on your Halloween costume."

Brandon glanced from Marin to Luke and appeared to judge that he was better off elsewhere. He scurried into another room. The walls were bright blue, and Luke caught a glimpse of white shelves before the door closed.

"He's never even met Cordy," said Marin. She pressed her fingers to her lips. "God, she's...she was sixteen. You've seen her, Detective. What did she look like? It's been three years, and she must have grown."

Luke reached into his jacket pocket and pulled out a piece of paper that had been folded at least four times. It was a photocopy of a freeze-frame from a security-camera feed. The Dusk Walkers were fast and could often sneak in and out of a shop without setting off the alarm.

It was only in the morning that the owners noticed things were missing and checked the cameras. He smoothed out the paper. The black-and-white photo was crumpled, but he could still see Cordy's face. He handed it to Marin. "Sorry, it's the clearest picture we could get from this year."

In the freeze-frame, Cordy sat atop Jack's shoulders. Her mouth was wide open in a hysterical laugh. One of her hands was in her friend's hair to keep her balance and the other made an obscene gesture at the camera. Jack lifted her closer to the camera, his hands gripping her ankles. He, too, was amused by the robbery they had just committed. His smile was frozen in a sideways grin, and his eyes were reduced to slits. Marin returned the photo to Luke, her face tight once more. "I would prefer to remember her as I knew her."

"Of course." He returned the paper to his pocket. "And whenever it's convenient for you, we'll need you to come down to the precinct to fill out some paperwork. I'm being reassigned, so you might not see me at all. Now that my job's done, I can't really continue a career as a 'Hunter.'"

Marin nodded curtly. He remembered the first time he met her and Richard, when they had visited him at the precinct to be introduced to the Hunters. Despite the fact that the separated couple had gone to meet the people who hunted their youngest daughter, both were polite and composed for the entire conference. Even now, as she processed Cordy's death, Marin was civil. "What will you do now?"

"I'll get my training as a real detective, and I might go

into organized crime," said Luke. He did not quite know what to add next. If he commented on how much more interesting the new job would be, it would be as though he did not care about Cordy. If he said that it would be boring, he could come off as being entertained by the Dusk Walkers.

His silence was not long enough to become awkward. Brandon the toddler waddled into the living room at that moment, dressed as a bumblebee. Marin gave a genuine laugh despite her red eyes, and Luke decided that he had no other reason to stay.

"Anyway, don't hesitate to call if you need anything," he said as he stood. "And don't forget to come to the precinct whenever you can."

"Yes, thank you, Detective." When she showed no signs of walking to the door with him, he smiled briefly at Brandon and left the apartment. The visit had not been as bad as he had been told, but he thought of the broken relationship between Marin and her daughter. Cordy had been away from her home for three years and had lost all memory of her family. Marin knew that, and she had perhaps convinced herself long ago that Cordy was gone.

Luke stood outside of the apartment and remembered the NYPD stationary that was stuffed in his pocket. He took it and peered at the writing he had left. Earlier, he had doubted that he would be able to deliver the message, but after meeting Cordy's mother, he was ready. He was ready to turn against his remaining superiors and side with the teenagers he had once called his enemies.

He called Gianna, and she answered immediately.

"Hey, you all right?"

"Fine." He started down the hall and pushed open the door to the staircase. "I just spoke to Mrs. Reid."

"How was she?"

"She took the news well. I mean, she wasn't happy about it, but she acted better than I expected. Anyway, I need to know Jack's location. You've still got the chip activated, right?"

"I do," said Gianna. She gave him an address. "Why?"

"I'll tell you when I get back," said Luke. He exited the building. "Love you."

"Okay." They hung up.

Ready to make a stop before his final destination, he pulled up Mr. Lear's address, hoping that he would take his daughter's death just as well as Marin. Somehow, he doubted that there would be waddling blond bumblebees there to cheer him up.

CHAPTER TWENTY TWO

The next thing Jack knew, Eva shook him awake. She stood over him, her hair hanging down with no restraint. He thought that strange because she usually wore her hair in a ponytail, even during the day. Jack sat up and rubbed the sleep out of his eyes nonetheless. It was his turn to keep watch.

"Get some rest," he said. He wanted to tell her something else, something important, but he could not quite remember...it was too early for thinking.

Eva straightened to leave, and he began to recall what he had meant to tell her, except that he was incapable of putting it into words. When she turned back to him, he prepared to speak what he had not yet considered.

Jack snapped his mouth shut when her fingers stroked his cheek. She leaned down, her pale lashes almost transparent when she closed her eyes. They kissed, and then he could no longer remember what he wanted to tell her. She tasted of berries, sweet and fresh and completely her. He had seen her chewing on flavored gum before, but she mostly did so during patrol when she thought that he was not looking. It would be their secret.

A familiar blast interrupted their moment, and his eyes opened with a jolt. Gunshots.

"You'll live forever," said Eva. Her eyes were no longer green, but white as snow. A dark-red bullet hole was directly in the middle of her forehead. Blood spouted from the wound, staining her pale skin. "But no one will remember your name."

"What?" His vision slid in and out of focus. Her voice echoed in his head.

"You'll never age, and you'll never die." Her lips were as red as the blood that still poured from her head. "Your friends will die soon, and then there will be no point in living. You'll spend eternity alone. You'll go insane."

Whatever she was, this was not real. Jack shook his head from right to left, but Eva remained in place. She raised a pistol that he had not noticed before and touched the tip to his forehead. Her white eyes would not leave him, even as he snapped upright on the sofa, shaking from head to toe.

"Jack?" said Cordy. "You okay?"

His best friend was in front of him now, and her eyes were the usual brown. "I—I'm fine," he said hoarsely, the taste of sleep still thick in his mouth.

"Sure. What's wrong?"

"What—no, I'm fine. I just had a nightmare, that's all." He heaved himself into a sitting position. Glancing at his wristwatch, he discovered that it was nearly six o'clock in the evening. "Have you been on patrol all day?"

She scoffed. "Here's the scoop: After I finished my shift, Eva took over. That was around noon. Then about a minute ago, she took the trouble of waking *me* up just so that *I* could wake *you* up. She must be really intent on avoiding you."

"That's what I tried to tell you." Jack opened his fists to run his hands through his messy hair, and he discovered a little ball of paper that rested in his palm.

"Maybe Eva left it there. Read it."

Jack smiled to himself, hoping that was true. He unfolded the paper and smoothed it out on his leg. It was a piece of stationary ripped from a notepad. The shield of the New York Police Department occupied a fraction of the heading. It was not from Eva.

'Meet us near the warehouse at 9:00 tonight. Avoid the cops and bring your friends. Just want to talk—Luke'

"What do you think he wants?" said Cordy.

Jack squished the paper in his fist and threw it across the floor. "It doesn't matter. We're not going."

"Why not?"

"Oh, I don't know!" he said with the heaviest sarcasm he could muster. "Maybe because the last two times I've met him, he wanted to kill us!"

"Don't you think that if he still wanted to kill us, he

would have done it at the warehouse? If not that, he definitely would have done it instead of leaving you a note. Luke's faster and stronger than all of us, which is probably how he got in. All he had to do was shoot Eva while she kept watch and kill the rest of us in our sleep."

Jack sucked his teeth while he waited for his mind to come up with an answer. Cordy had a point. "Fine. Let's say that he doesn't want to kill us. What does he want?"

She pointed at the paper ball. "He wrote that he just wants to talk."

"Duh, I know that's what he wrote. What does he really want?"

"Why does he have to have an ulterior motive?"

"Because I don't trust the guy who shot me in the face, thank you very much." Jack pulled his knees to his chest. "We're not going."

"You guys talk really loudly," said Lily. She, Eva, and Alix walked out of the adjoining room, rubbing the sleep from their eyes. "We're right here, you know."

"Sorry." Cordy shrugged in apology, and Jack had nothing to add. "It's just that Jack has this thing—"

He kicked her in the ribs with his foot to shut her up. Cordy snatched up the ball of paper anyway and tossed it to Lily. Jack rolled off of the couch too slowly and was not quick enough to catch the note in its flight. Even if he had managed to grab it, the four girls would not leave him alone until it was read.

"Look at that," said Lily when she finished reading the note. "Jack just got asked on his first date!" The silly grin on her face only grew when he scowled at her.

Eva snatched the paper from her hands, and she and Alix read it together. "Are we going?" said the youngest Dusk Walker.

"No," said Jack without hesitation. He predicted what she would say next. "And just because he says that he's with us now, that doesn't mean that we can trust him. It could be a trick."

"We can at least go see what he wants," said the ever-curious Lily. "If he had wanted to hurt us, he could have done it when we were asleep. Instead, he left a note."

"That's what I told him." Cordy's smirk was an invitation for one of his killer glares, which seemed to have no effect on any of the girls. As Jack brooded, the four other Dusk Walkers chattered on about Luke's note.

He secured his knife to his belt and climbed to his feet. "Fine. You win. We'll find out what he wants, but I'm going alone."

"What?" said Cordy, her eyes reduced to slits of accusation. "Have you forgotten what happened the last time you went off on your own?"

Her words stopped him in his tracks. By the pointed look in her glare, he knew that she was not referring to his death. She meant something so much more important and valuable. Alix ducked her head, for Cordy was talking about how the youngster's life had been put in danger.

Jack had not linked his previous departure with her kidnapping until then. He was so selfish, so reckless to have done that to his youngest friend, and that he had not connected the two events before Cordy's mention made the situation ten times worse. "I'm sorry, Al."

Jack knelt beside her and hugged her tightly. Her pointy chin impaled his shoulder, but he did not care. Her tears were his own stupid fault, and he had to pay the price. "Promise you won't leave again."

"I promise," he said. The pledge was not only for her. From then on, he swore to himself that he would never abandon his friends again. They were a team, and they would face their conflicts together. It went completely against his nature, but he would give the plan his best effort. "And I guess we can all visit Luke together. Lily, get the map."

Alix stopped crying, and Lily rushed back to her room to retrieve her backpack. While Cordy attempted to peel a beaming Alix off of Jack, he spotted another smile in front of him: Eva. Cordy whisked Alix from the room and shut the door behind them as they joined Lily. "Hi."

Jack's palms were sweating. He wiped them awkwardly on his jeans. "Yeah—I mean, hey."

Eva's smile fell, and she avoided his eyes. "Good job with Alix."

"I do what I can." He gave a shrug as if to say that he couldn't help it. "Good job ignoring me for no reason."

When he saw the way her eyebrows raised, he knew

that he had said the wrong thing.

"Sorry. And, um, so I guess you do…have feelings…"

"Just because I'm a girl doesn't mean I don't have feelings." Eva folded her arms over her chest and narrowed her eyes. He felt chastised, and he rubbed the back of his neck, which had surely turned as red as a fire engine. It had never been this hard to talk to her, not when they first met and not even lately, when he understood how he felt.

"You're not making this very easy," he said. His tongue was heavy now, and his words turned into slurs. He might as well get what he wanted to say over with before he turned into complete mush. "I meant…you have feelings…for me?"

"I guess I do." Her hands gripped her elbows tightly, and she did not look happier. In fact she seemed almost as miserable as she had been in the moments after his death. "What about you?"

"Oh, I'm in love with my sense of humor and my good looks," said Jack. His confidence had taken a jetpack and soared above his head when she confirmed what Cordy had told him. Eva's forehead creased, and she frowned. Again, he had used the wrong words. "I mean, yeah. Ev, I really meant it earlier when I said that I love you. I have since, literally, as long as I can remember."

The anxiety in her face relaxed as she exhaled and smiled. His head buzzed in glee, denying all possibility that this was another dream that would soon go bad. His mind was not cruel enough to play that trick on him.

"Cool," she said, voicing his thoughts. "How about after our deal with Luke is done, we hop over to the nearest grocery store and snag a container of ice cream?"

He almost rushed forward to kiss her, longing to taste her lips again. However, he knew that this was the wrong moment. Later, when they would steal the ice cream, he would consider kissing her. He and Luke still had unfinished business that he would take care of with his truest friends.

Eva pulled him into the room where Cordy, Lily, and Alix hid. "Have you figured out how we're getting back to the warehouse?"

Lily lifted the map, and Jack could distinguish a circle of black marker in the south of District Two. She had traced a line that led from their current location to the warehouse they wanted to reach. "It's too far to walk, and we can't risk the subway now that we're dead. I suggest we steal a car."

Eva nodded. "Let's do it."

They packed their bags and made their way out of the ramshackle house. Once they were outside, they only had to turn the corner before they came upon several cars parked along the sidewalk. Searching for the reason behind the accumulation, Jack found a banner that floated just over their heads that read, 'Hotel.' He heard voices nearby and located a middle-aged couple. The man, balding and pot-bellied, rolled the woman's suitcase across the asphalt of the parking lot. They walked toward the Dusk Walkers, unaware.

"Boring trip?" said the man. He lifted a set of keys and pushed a button. A small blue car ahead let out a sharp beep as it unlocked. Jack peered at the license plate, which originated from Maine. It was possible that the man and woman did not know much about the Dusk Walkers.

"Boring trip," agreed the woman. "Thanks for coming to get me. You know how I hate public transportation."

The couple arrived on the sidewalk. They were still yards away from the car and had not seen the children, even as the group retreated back around the corner. Jack made a series of hand signals. First, he pointed at Cordy, Eva, and Lily. He jerked his thumb toward the couple. Next, he motioned for Alix to get onto his back. He pulled his hood over his head as she prepared to jump. They had done this procedure dozens of times. Although it was fun, they would have to be more cautious than ever. He did not know if the news of their death had spread yet.

Lily fumbled awkwardly with the waistline of her pants. There was a second's pause, then a long furry tail sprouted from her lower back. Alix wrapped her arms around Jack's neck, and he lifted her off of the ground. They were ready.

Cordy, Eva, and Lily ran toward the couple while Jack and Alix crossed the street. He jogged past a thin line of trees, stepping carefully as the girl on his back made airplane noises. They both laughed, attracting the man and woman's attention. The couple paused to look at the boy and the girl, who could have passed as siblings. In their distraction, three teenage girls were able to get closer to them. Jack slowed and watched Cordy crash into the woman.

"Sorry!" She faked distress. "I'm so sorry, ma'am, I'm such a klutz."

Eva was beside the driver's door of the blue car. While the balding man turned to help his wife, Lily took the opportunity to spare him of his keys with her prehensile tail. This was the most difficult part of the trick. She caught the keys in her hand and threw them to Eva. Eva opened the door, put the key into the ignition and started the car while Cordy and Lily leapt inside. Naturally, the couple did not stand still. Jack accelerated his run at the same time as the man. "Hey! Get the hell back here!"

Alix released her grip and ran alongside Jack. Eva would not stop until she reached a safe distance from the couple. The runners sprinted several blocks before the blue car finally slowed. Out of breath and with a stitch in his side, Jack dared to glance back. The man was not fast enough and had fallen behind, and his wife was even farther away. "You okay?" he said to Alix.

"Yeah..." She massaged a spot under her ribs. "I'm...fine."

Cordy pushed open the door for them. The car had not even come to a full stop when Jack and Alix clambered into the back seat. Cordy sat in the left seat, and Lily was on the right. He allowed the middle seat to go to Alix while he climbed into the passenger seat. Eva did not wait for him to sit before she pressed on the gas pedal.

"For a moment there, I thought you'd never stop." He yanked off his hood and settled his windblown hair.

"Of course I would," said Eva. She kept her eyes on the road as she turned onto the bridge. "I could never leave Alix."

CHAPTER TWENTY THREE

Eva parked two blocks away from their destination. The car faced the direction from where they came. Outside of his window, Jack was face to face with a laundromat. The blue-and-white banner above the door suggested that he drop off his clothes for the dry cleaning services. "This isn't the warehouse."

She shook her head, leaving the keys in the ignition. "If they find the car, they won't know where we went. It's safer that way. And just in case…" She shrugged off her thin sweater and used the fabric to wipe the steering wheel. "Erase your fingerprints."

Jack had hardly touched anything. With his sleeve, he rubbed the inner door handle and the plastic around it. He stepped outside of the car when Eva did, and they scrubbed at the outer door handles. Cordy, Lily, and Alix followed suit.

"I almost forgot," he said. They left the car by the sidewalk and walked toward the warehouse. He could still smell smoke in the air. "I need a new backpack. Maybe we could stop somewhere on the way back."

"Sure." Eva turned on the spot, peering at street signs

and buildings. Her brow furrowed, and he knew what she was thinking. "Wait a second, I know this place. Alix, do you know what happened here?"

Alix shook her head. Jack could not answer the question either, for their surroundings were unfamiliar to him. He listened to what Eva said next.

"Okay, so many years ago, there was a parade on this street with a bunch of cops. As the story goes, people in the buildings started shooting. The mafia was suspected, but no one was ever caught."

"Unsolved deaths." Cordy skipped down the sidewalk with a whimsical smile. "My favorite! You know, I could be a great homicide cop. I would just go up to the body, call the ghost, and ask who killed them. Problem solved."

A gunshot rang through the air, and Lily screamed. Jack recognized the sound of a pistol and not a sniper's rifle. The shooter's aim would be less precise, but it still presented a danger. He knew that it was not Roy, who would not have decided to use a handgun if he still chose to attack from a distance. Jack whirled around, making sure that his friends were unharmed. The only damage that the bullet had done was a dent in the sidewalk behind them.

His eyes darted around the street, his peripheral vision blurring. He could not focus on anything, least of all the shooter. It was a long avenue with several windows and flat rooftops. Their assailant could be anywhere.

Cordy grabbed his wrist and yelled. He only heard a dull shout.

"What?" he said, stumbling after her when she dragged him away.

"Run!"

Eva was already halfway to the next strip of sidewalk. Between where he stood and the concrete ahead, there was a road that led to Jack's left. He came close to leading the girls down that path before he spotted the yellow sign that read, 'Dead End.'

They were almost across the street when the yellow sign in front of them was shot. The blast echoed from a different direction. There was more than one shooter, and they intended to trap the Dusk Walkers. Thinking swiftly, Jack took the hand closest to his, Cordy's, and turned left.

"But it's a dead end!" She pointed at the pierced sign.

"It's better than standing there and getting shot!" The girls followed him. The small street was perfectly straight, with apartments and empty sidewalks framing the asphalt. At the far end of the short road, conveniently labeled 'End,' he saw a short brick wall that had seen better days. Eight openings that served as windows were positioned in a row on the wall. They were low enough for the five of them to jump through. If they were safe from the shooters, escape would be easy.

As Jack's eyes fully relieved themselves of the tunnel vision that he had experienced, he came to a halt. A fence rose behind the wall, blocking off the windows. He let out several curses and combed back his hair, turning on the spot. His head pounded with questions, and he had time for none of them.

"Jack," said Eva. She looked up, but not at the wall in search for a way out. She faced instead toward the fire escapes on the sides of the buildings.

People stood on the metal landings. Jack counted several dozens of them. They all wore dark clothes, which made it more difficult to see them in the dimly lit street. There were so many of them, all climbing down the fire escapes to reach the Dusk Walkers. He squinted to look at their faces and recognized several of them as Nor'easters. Among the dozens of strangers he saw Tempest, Squall, Cyclone, and Thunderhead. Zephyr, whom Jack had left in the holding cells of an unknown police station, was absent.

"Back from the dead, are we?" said Squall, his fedora ragged as ever and his suit slightly less cheap. He carried a wooden baseball bat in his hands. The rest of the group also carried bats, or were armed with knives, guns, and brass knuckles.

Cordy took a step forward. Jack pulled at her sleeve, but she did not stop until she stood in front of Thunderhead. The dark-skinned teen hugged herself, clearly ill at ease. "Thunder...baby, it's me."

Thunderhead's pierced nostrils flared, and she stepped backward. "You were dead. Everyone's heard."

"Obviously it's not true," said Cordy. "Well, Jack was dead for a few minutes, but that's a completely different story."

"No one cares!" said Squall. He raised his bat. "All I wanna know is how much we'll get for turning 'em in!"

He swung the weapon, barely missing Lily's head. Without a second thought, Jack drew his knife and lunged at his former ally. The two young men crashed into the brick wall of an apartment building, and Squall's baseball bat clattered to the ground. In the form of a tiger, Lily picked it up in her jaws and snapped the weapon in two as though it were a breadstick.

Three strangers approached Cordy and Alix with brass knuckles. They held the enemies at bay with their own sharp elbows and quick movements. Eva, on the other hand, fought ten of the gang members at once, including Cyclone and Tempest. She turned their own weapons against some of them and disarmed others completely. Grabbing onto the bottom of the fire escape ladder, she hoisted herself into the air and smashed her foot into a man's nose. He collapsed, and she dropped lightly back onto the ground. She had hardly broken a sweat when she pulled herself into a fighting stance.

Squall's ribs snapped when Lily leaned a paw on his chest. When the man was rendered incapable of sitting up, Jack knelt beside him and narrowed his eyes. "You sold us out, didn't you? Who are these other people?"

Squall tried to move, and Jack put his knife close to the man's eye. The Dusk Walker set his jaw, staring down at the gang member. The man in the suit did not know Jack well. He did not know that Jack would not hurt him.

"Why don't you just answer the question?" Jack cocked an eyebrow and grinned at his knife. Its blade glimmered even in the dark, happy to be put to use. It reflected something, perhaps a streetlight from beyond the dead end. He shifted until he was closer to Squall, and so was the knife.

"Wait, don't!" said the fedora-sporting man. His hat had been knocked off during the fall. It lay only feet away, so tempting to wear. It would be a reminder of Jack's success. "Fine. We spotted you at one o' your ol' hiding spots, and we tracked you over here. Us Nor'easters ain't enough to take you down, so we asked some other guys to help. They're pros."

"Pros?"

"Yeah, they're right behind ya."

Jack made the mistake of turning around. A set of brass knuckles charged at him, and his nose snapped with a stabbing crackle.

It was as if his face were on fire. He could not see, and the sounds around him were muffled. The single punch had left him laying on his back and bleeding profusely from his nose.

"Stings, don't it?" said a deep voice that he did not recognize. "Get him up."

Jack's eyes darted from left to right, and he saw various pairs of baggy jeans and sweatpants, but the orange of Lily's tiger form was absent. Strong hands pulled him into a kneeling position and slid his knife from his belt. As Jack's full vision returned, he found himself staring at a pair of suede shoes.

"Lift his head," said the strange voice, muffled to Jack's ears. The thug who held his left arm grabbed a fistful of his bloody hair, wrenching it backward until Jack looked to the sky. A man in a dark-grey suit stood in front of him. Jack blinked the red from his eyes. His face itched as the wounds healed gradually. The suited man had a strangely boyish face, with smooth skin and bright eyes, an unidentifiable evil radiating off of him. The man leaned down and took Jack's chin between two careful fingers. "Incredible."

He licked his thumb and dragged it across Jack's cheekbone, wiping away the blood there as though he did so every day.

"Not even a scar..." The man gaped in awe. "You impossible creature. How could we ever turn you in?"

Jack swallowed hard. He did not know what was worse: ending up in the government's test lab or in the clutches of the New York street gangs. He would rather die, but he could not do that either.

He craned his neck around, praying that his friends were better off than him. Cordy was thrust to the ground by Thunderhead, and she hit the asphalt with a guttural gasp, but she appeared unharmed. The fall had been a short one, and she was tough.

"We can't turn him in. We would gain almost no profit if we did that, compared to what would come from keeping him. We would be richer than the mafia."

While the thugs marveled at the idea, Jack could only dread the outcome of the evening. He drew his brows together, and Eva looked his way. He knew that she was smart enough to know that he was not a priority. If his throat was slit, he would only be gone for a few minutes before he woke up once more. The other Dusk Walkers did not own that luxury.

"And the girls?" said the man to Jack's right. Eva's punch landed in a thug's throat, and he backed away from little Alix, who was helpless when she was unable to retrieve her fire. Tempest rose to the challenge, her dark-red ponytail dancing to and fro. She cried out as Eva twisted her arm in a way that could not be pleasant.

"Nah, they'd put up too much of a fight," said the man in the suit. "Turner can heal if we break his nose, but he doesn't have anything that's useful in combat, unlike the rest. I hate to say it, but let's let the government take care of them."

Jack's attention returned to the conversation, and his insides boiled with rage. He had promised not to abandon his friends. Even if someone attempted to force them apart, he would never let them go.

Doubtful of what damage he could do, Jack spotted his knife in the hands of the thug on his left, and he lunged, taking the men by surprise. He slipped from their grips, and his fingers brushed the handle of his weapon briefly before a set of brass knuckles struck his cheek. He grunted, and his shoulder crunched against the asphalt. His knife was gone. Dizzy beyond relief and seeing stars, Jack could only let himself be held down again, this time by four men.

"If you try something like that again, I won't hesitate to put you down like a mad dog." The suited man pressed the muzzle of a gun to Jack's temple. "Army would probably find something to do with you anyway. Is that what you want?"

Jack could only laugh, despite knowing that he looked like a maniac, with blood still trickling from his nose and drying on his cheek. This stranger could not threaten him with death, nor could anyone else.

"What?" said the gang member, certainly high on the hierarchal pyramid because of his fancy clothes. The flare of his nostrils gave away his bluff. Jack had successfully thrown him off of his pedestal. "What's so funny?"

"No, it's just that..." He laughed again. "Nothing."

The man in the suit frowned and struck him across his temple with the butt of his gun. Jack saw stars and heard the familiar blast of a gunshot. Disoriented once more, he took longer to recover. It took him several seconds to realize that he was uninjured. When he deduced that the bullet had not been fired from the suited man's gun, he looked up.

CHAPTER TWENTY FOUR

"Ah, the cavalry!" Jack grinned again. The repeated blows to his face had bewildered his thought process, but through a healing black eye he recognized the man he was supposed to meet. For once, he was glad to see Luke. "Book 'em, Danno."

"Christian Knight, also known as Prince Charming. Known gang member. You're under arrest for racketeering, extortion, murder, and a whole lot of other crap." Luke pointed his pistol at the groaning figure of the man in the suit, who lay on the ground as he clutched the wound in his leg. Luke then turned to the thugs who held Jack. "Let him go. You're under arrest too, but I'll get to you later."

Jack felt the four men hesitate before releasing their grips. He stumbled across the damp asphalt to lean against the wall as his head spun. Time seemed frozen around him. Luke kept the thugs at gunpoint, Cordy was still pinned down by Thunderhead, Eva held several gang members at bay while they stared at the Hunter, Lily's gigantic paw kept Tempest horizontal while the tiger awaited Luke's orders, and Alix had climbed up a broken fire escape, flames in her hands. Several men and women were on the ground, either unconscious or wounded. Jack suspected that Eva was responsible for most of them.

While everyone was silent apart from the odd moan of discomfort, footsteps approached. Carrying numerous sets of handcuffs, Gianna ran into the dead end. Her hair was in a loose bun, and dark strands were caught in her eyelashes. Rae followed silently behind.

Luke was closest to Gianna. She stood on the tips of her toes to whisper in his ear. Jack watched, awaiting an explanation. Luke glanced around the street, shifting his weight from foot to foot. Finally, he spoke to Jack.

"Carefully, very carefully, the five of you are going to get out of here. Climb up the fire escapes and get onto the roofs. A ton of cops are already on their way. This is a big catch."

Jack nodded hastily and scooped up his knife from the ground. As he crossed the street, he gestured for Alix to come down from the fire escape. The thugs below were red with rage when they were forced to move out of the way. Jack could not resist the comment that he would make.

"Sucks, doesn't it?" he said to the nearest gang member.

"What?" The man was not much older than him. He wore no shirt under his leather jacket, which stank of rotten bananas.

Jack lifted his arms to help guide Alix onto solid ground. She stayed close to him like a magnet, moving when he did. "Y'all are stuck in your own trap."

The banana man's square eyebrows crawled together on his forehead to form one large black caterpillar. "Trap?"

"Oh, you know…" Jack wiggled his fingers dramatically. "The dead end!"

The man scowled and looked as though he would pounce. Knowing that the gangster was unable of trying anything without the Hunters taking him down, Jack blew out his tongue in a raspberry.

"Kid," called Luke. Pulling his tongue back into his mouth, Jack turned around. He shrugged as if to say, "What?" Luke shook his head. "Don't do that."

He glared. It had been silently agreed that they were no longer enemies, but that did not give Luke the right to act as though he were a normal police officer and Jack were a normal teenager. Nonetheless, he stepped away from the banana man. If Luke's words were to be trusted, real authorities would arrive at any moment.

Eva and Lily came to join him and Alix, gang members cursing at them as they walked. He helped Cordy to her feet, and Thunderhead backed toward the wall. The two girls had never had a serious relationship to his knowledge, but they were surely close. It was just like any other breakup, except it involved superpowers and gangs. Jack had to respect that, despite the grief-ridden look on Cordy's face. He did not want her to be sad.

"You all right?" He tried to follow Eva as she headed out of the dead end, but Cordy would not budge. The heels of her hands were at her temples, and tears filled her eyes. This did not have anything to do with Thunderhead; he knew that much. "Dee, what's going on?"

She whimpered. "Th—they're too strong. Too many of 'em, can't hold 'em back…"

"Hold who back?"

Eva understood before him. She mouthed something that he could not decipher. He did not care; he only wanted to know what was wrong with Cordy.

"Ghost cops," hissed Eva when he did nothing. "From the parade massacre!"

At first, Jack did not know what she meant. He had experienced many strange dealings with life and death in recent hours, but he did not remember a parade, nor a massacre. It took a short moment for it to dawn on him. Earlier, Eva had mentioned a shooting that had happened a few years ago in the street nearby, where unknown suspects killed a group of police officers. Before that, before he went to visit his father, he had heard the man on the bench mention the tragedy's anniversary. The ghosts of the officers would return to solve their own cold case.

Jack left Cordy in Eva's care and jabbed his knife at Squall's face. The fedora was already back on the hooligan's head. "You killed all those cops?"

"Years ago," wheezed Squall. He clutched his broken ribs. "It was part of my initiation. Am I supposed to give a damn?"

"You should. This is your just deserts." This was perfect retribution for the sudden rupture of their alliance. The Nor'easters could not be allowed to roam free with the knowledge that the Dusk Walkers were alive. He looked to Luke, who was occupied with restraining the conscious thugs from the other gang. He and Gianna were unaware of Cordy's warning. "And what about these other guys? The ones that aren't Nor'easters?"

"Some of 'em were there, yeah." Squall squared his shoulders and looked away, deciding that Jack had heard too much. "Why?"

"Jack..." Cordy sat on the ground, her knees pulled to her chest. "They're coming now. I can't stop them."

"Will they hurt us?" said Eva.

The Ghost-Whisperer shook her head. "Only those who wronged them. I can keep the eight of us safe."

Jack exchanged glances with Luke across the street. Cordy wanted to protect the Hunters, which he would have never tried if he had her ability. He knew that if he had the choice, he would not waste his energy on their three former enemies.

Except they had done the same for him. Luke had come to his rescue, this time with nothing to gain. In the warehouse, he had only worked with the Dusk Walkers in order to escape, using Alix's power. Now, Luke was putting himself and his friends in danger. Not only did the two gangs outnumber them, but the aftermath of the evening would end with Luke in a tight spot. The gangsters would claim that they had seen the five children who were meant to be dead and that the Hunters had been involved. The city surely already distrusted the three detectives, due to the lack of bodies found at the warehouse. Even if they did manage to apprehend a couple dozen gang members, the consequences that would ensue would not make the arrest worthwhile. He had never imagined that the thought would ever cross his mind, but he trusted Luke.

"What the hell was that?" Squall's face was grey, whether from pain or from fear, Jack did not know. He only gripped the handle of his knife with sweating fingers.

The ground trembled. Those who were on the ground leapt to their feet. Streetlamps flickered, and Gianna's hand flew protectively to her stomach. Luke's arm encircled her, and Rae vanished. Her feet were the only ones that dared to move. Jack could hear her run past him and up a fire-escape ladder across the street. He looked at the two remaining detectives, who did not appear to have noticed.

"Al, go up that fire escape." He pointed to a red ladder that seemed intact. Rae was clever. He did not know what she was up to, but she had given him an idea to protect his friends. "Get as high as you can and don't look down." Jack helped Eva pull down the ladder for Alix to start climbing.

"That ain't what you're supposed to do in an earthquake!" Squall stood, doubled over because of his ribs. "Are you all idiots?"

"This isn't an earthquake," said Jack. "And we're not

the idiots; you are."

Alix was already at the third landing when the screams began. Jack slapped his palms over his ears and dropped to his knees, his eyes squeezing shut. These were no worldly sounds. The screeches were over quickly, and silence echoed in his ears. As he discovered upon looking around him, he was not the only one who had ended up on the ground. Although the phenomenon was unprecedented for him, he took a wild guess and presumed that the ghosts had arrived.

He was right.

On the street that led to the dead end, the roads shuddered and split. Out of the crater rose columns of smoke as thick as trees.

The ground no longer trembled, but Jack's hands would not stop shaking. The dead frightened him just as much as losing his friends. These ghosts had been forced from life, forced away from their families and into the limbo state in which they were stranded. Their murders had not even been with a cause. It was for sport, for a stupid initiation into a gang. They certainly had reason to be angry with their killers.

As the phantoms condensed into humanoid figures, Jack counted over thirty police officers in ceremonial uniform. They marched into the dead end, carrying rifles over their shoulders. Cordy had once told him that weapons did not work for ghosts, but they had other ways of taking their revenge.

Cyclone stumbled forward, yielding a baseball bat. Jack

knew that the blond man would not be a target of the ghosts, being the newest recruit into the Nor'easters. The parade massacre had happened years ago. However, he had made the mistake that cost him his life. Perhaps if he had stayed put, he would have survived.

Cyclone charged at the specters, swinging at the first officer with a battle cry. The baseball bat did not harm the ghost whatsoever, and the thug fell through the phantom's body. The dead officer snapped Cyclone's neck before he even hit the ground.

The remaining gangsters yelled and darted every which way. Some tried to attack the ghosts and failed, and others attempted to run up the fire-escape ladders. They, too, were apprehended, and their necks were snapped. Those who had already been restrained by the Hunters were killed on the spot.

When the adversaries began to understand that the ghosts could not be attacked, they turned instead against the Dusk Walkers. Tempest swung her brass knuckles at Jack, the weapon on her left hand. He had seen earlier that she was right-handed, but Eva had injured her arm.

Jack ducked from the punch and swept his knife at her leg, which was exposed under a pair of tight-fitting shorts. He did not aim to kill. The ghosts were there for that. Tempest cried out and grabbed his arm for support, her oily bangs falling over her eyes. He tried to shake her off, then she rammed her left fist into his abdomen.

Blinking back tears, he kicked off the wall and lunged at the traitor. They both crashed onto the asphalt, but the fight was over before he had expected. A silvery man in a dark uniform crouched at Tempest's side and grabbed a fistful of her hair with one hand, then cupped her chin with the other. He twisted hard, and the crunch that followed made Jack want to turn over and empty his stomach onto the asphalt.

The ghost did not even glance his way before soaring to kill again. Jack propped himself up on his elbows and looked at Tempest. Her neck was torn at an angle that was impossible to survive. For a split second, she struggled to breathe and then stopped moving. Blood stained the black of the road. Her eyes were already glassy, and her irises were darker and bluer than they normally appeared.

He had wanted her dead. He had been glad that a ghost would take care of his dirty work for him. Looking at her now, he saw that she was just as human as him, if not more so.

"Turner," said a voice to his left. Jack whirled around, only for a baseball bat to strike the back of his head.

The next few moments were a blur of white-hot agony. He was sure that he had very briefly lost consciousness, because when he opened his eyes, he was on his back. He looked up at a hatless Squall, whose hands were around Jack's throat.

"I'm the traitor, eh? I called on a few ol' friends to help save my own skin. Ya little punks hired cops and goddamned ghosts to kill us!" Squall squeezed harder. Jack's arms flailed uselessly, pinned down at the elbows by Squall's knees. He could not kick his legs high enough to push off Squall. His eyes swam with tears, and his heart gave a violent kick. His blood pounded in his head, and heat flushed his cheeks. His brain needed oxygen. "I was never gonna kill ya. That was never how it was gonna go down. If you'd cooperated, this could've all been very simple. No one could've gotten hurt. But o' course, ya screwed that up. And everyone's dead."

Jack glanced to the side to see if all of his enemies were truly dead, and he only saw cloudy movements. Squall, whose squinty eyes were mere inches away, was the only figure he could recognize.

"Again, I didn't want it to come to this." Squall leaned the rest of his weight onto Jack's throat.

He felt as though his head would explode. His eyes rolled backward into his skull, and the wailing in his ears was surely from the lack of oxygen. This death would not be as quick as the one Luke had caused.

Then he had air. A great weight lifted from his chest, and Squall was gone. Jack was dragged backward, or the asphalt moved forward, as his sight began to clear. His vision filled with spots of red and green amongst the black. He gulped in wheezing breaths of air, his mind lightheaded as oxygenated blood rushed to his brain.

Squall yelled, and Jack knew what the wailing sounds were. The ghosts had saved Squall for last. They did not give him a quick death by snapping his neck like the other gangsters. Instead, a half dozen specters knelt around Squall. Jack could no longer see the fedora-loving man, but the rusty stench of blood floated toward him, and he knew that the ghosts had taken their revenge.

He drew in a hissing breath. He had wished for justice to be served, but he had not wished that much pain on anyone. Squall still screamed. Jack knew that he only had moments left, judging by the amount of blood everywhere. The ghosts began to dissipate, and he looked away at first, not at all in a hurry to see what they had done to the body.

He had been too distracted to realize that someone sat next to him. Luke gawked at Squall, his nose wrinkled in disgust. His hand still gripped Jack's shoulder, which he had been oblivious to until that moment. Jack did not look at the dead Nor'easter, but instead at the Hunter, who had pulled him out from under Squall. For the second time that evening and the third time that day, Luke had saved him.

Jack stared for too long. Like the Dusk Walker, Luke had been too occupied with Squall's death to notice anything else.

"Sorry." Removing his hand from Jack's shoulder, he turned to his other side, returning with the boy's knife. Jack had dropped it when he and Tempest fell.

"Thanks," he said, something he never thought he would utter honestly to Luke. He had expected to feel a twisting feeling of wrong in his gut, but the word had come out with no guilt whatsoever.

Jack put the knife in his belt and finally looked to Squall. He now felt nauseated, and not because of Luke. The ghosts had torn the Nor'easter to pieces, each of his limbs separate from his torso. His head still remained attached to his neck, but his eyes were gouged out, nowhere to be seen. Many vital organs lay in the road. Intestines snaked into a mess similar to a bowl of spaghetti. A lumpy heart lay to Squall's right, next to what Jack thought could be a lung.

CHAPTER TWENTY FIVE

Jack looked away from Squall and spotted Alix on a metal landing near the top of the fire escape, her face buried in her hands. He did not know if she hid from the sounds that she had heard or from the sight of the body, but at least she was safe.

Luke was on his feet in a second. He extended his hand toward Jack, who let himself be helped to his feet. "You all right?" said the Hunter when Jack stumbled.

"Fine." He rubbed his aching temples. "Just my head."

The blares of police sirens did not help soothe his oxygen-deprived head. Real living police officers were on their way. Luke gave him a small shove. "You need to go right now. Get to the roof. I'll meet you there soon."

Jack turned around and spotted Cordy already climbing up the fire-escape ladder. He guessed that the small brown bird that fluttered toward the roof was Lily. As for Eva, her feet were still on the ground.

Gianna stood over a member of the second gang, whose neck was intact. She secured his hands behind his back. Five others remained breathing, including two whom he recognized from the Nor'easters. Prince Charming was also unharmed, apart from the wound in his leg. He scowled at Jack from across the street.

Eva pulled herself up the ladder with strength and agility that he could never have. She squatted down on the landing and reached toward him. There was a small cut on her cheek, but otherwise she seemed healthy. Relieved, he took her hand, and she pulled him upward until he was able to get his feet onto the ladder. After that, it was simple. They hurried up stairs until they arrived on a landing, scuttled around pots and plants, then continued up the next set of steps. It was as though there were a fire, but the procedure was in reverse.

They came to the top landing, and Jack glanced down. Luke and Gianna were dots from afar. A row of arrestees knelt on the sidewalk. The bodies of the fallen lay scattered on the streets, and Squall's stood out the most. He was blood red among black and grey ants.

The first police car arrived just as Eva tapped his shoulder. She had already climbed onto the roof and reached for him again. He stood on the fence surrounding the landing and pushed off with his foot, making it easier for her to pull him up.

Jack wanted to look down again in order to see what was happening, but arms embraced him in a tight hug before he had even gotten to his feet.

"I'm glad you're okay," said Eva. Her jaw moved against his shoulder as she spoke. Some of her hair had caught in his mouth, not bothering him whatsoever. He smiled, simply glad that he was worthy of her affection. "I saw that you were in trouble, but more guys attacked Cordy and me. At least Luke was there to help you out."

"Yeah." He returned the hug. "Thank God for Luke."

She scoffed and brought her arms back to her sides. A whimsical grin was on her lips when she weaved her fingers between his. Eva turned around, and she went to join the others. Jack followed her. "You know you love him."

His eyes widened. "No!"

"Shh!" She whirled around, a finger pressed to her lips. He soon saw what she did and forgot all about Luke. Jack and Eva released each other's hands as they approached the singular sight.

Cordy stood near the center of the roof. Alix was close behind her with a brown sparrow perched on her shoulder. In front of the three girls was a mass of translucent grey. The ghosts had returned.

"If you want," Cordy said to the dead officer in the front. "We could ask the two detectives who helped us if they could legally solve your murders. Now that they know who did it, it'll be easier to find evidence, won't it?"

The uniformed phantom shook his head. "The Hunters already have enough on their plate. There's no need to make them even more suspicious. Our deaths were avenged. That's what we all needed."

"Does this mean you can move on? Is it enough?" Jack saw the strain of tears in Cordy's voice. She truly cared about the ghosts, as though even after all the bloodshed, they were her friends.

The ghosts nodded, forming a wave of nodding silver police officers. "Goodbye, Miss Lear. And you're welcome."

The forms of the dead soon lost their solidity. It began with the fading of their outlines, and then they returned to the columns of smoke that had risen from the crack in the road. This time, they faded upward and into the air, toward the sky. They were now at peace. Jack had never enjoyed the presence of Cordy's ghosts, but this time he was sad to see them go. Not only would they have been helpful in a fight, but they were some of the nicer police officers that he had met, in their own special way.

Cordy wiped away her tears with the back of her sleeve, and blood came away with it. Lily returned to her human form, and her hairline was caked with red. When he asked if they were all right, they nodded. "D'you think that Prince Charming and the others will convince the cops that we're alive?" he said.

"The Hunters' word is more reliable than the ones of convicted criminals," said Lily. "So I doubt it."

"What about all of the bodies?" Cordy gestured toward the dead end. "How will they explain those?"

"We won't."

Jack turned around. Luke had appeared on the rooftop without a sound. He strode toward the Dusk Walkers, his hands in his pockets and a smile lifting the corners of his lips. "Tonight at nine o'clock, Gee and I visited the warehouse to see how the investigation was going. We decided to walk back to our apartment, and we got an anonymous call telling us to come here. Before complying, we called the organized-crime precinct. We came here, found the bodies and the other guys, and that's all we know. Gianna's telling them that story right now. And I left to take a breather because as we all know, I don't like dead bodies."

"You're going to lie," deduced Lily. She narrowed her eyes. "First you lied that we're dead, and you're gonna do it again?"

"I've been spreading lies all day. I think I can spare a few more. Moving on…" Luke fumbled in his pocket and pulled out a wad of cash. "Here. Take it and get out of my city."

"What?"

"You can't risk being seen at all. You have a better chance of going unnoticed if you aren't in New York, where people will recognize you. Go to Union City, Jersey City, wherever. Just don't stay here."

When Jack did not move, Eva stepped forward and took the cash. "Thank you."

"If you're going to leave, I don't want to be the one responsible for a rise in break-ins in some other city. That'll last you a while."

Eva pocketed the money, and Jack had more questions.

"What about Rae?" he said. "I saw her run up here, then she was gone."

Luke shrugged. "I have no clue where she is, but she didn't want to be here. She hasn't spoken to me all day, and when she's forced to communicate, she just nods her head. Letting you guys live was never her plan. I guess she isn't a fan of lying."

"I thought you were friends."

"We were." Luke nodded. "She was solitary, though, and Gee and I had to work with her. She never really fit in. I guess letting you live was the final straw for her. I can only hope that she hasn't gone to help Roy."

"Good riddance to her if she has." Jack did not doubt the loyalty of his four friends or of the twins. He trusted them with his life.

"Hold your horses, she's still my partner." Luke gave a short chuckle. When it was over, he looked at the five teenagers with a careful eye and took a cautious step forward. "Listen, speaking of friends—"

"No," said Jack. He took a step backward, landing on Cordy's foot.

"No?"

"No, we won't be your friends." Luke had saved him many times, and Jack did not acknowledge it. He felt guilty for a moment before he continued talking. "What you've done for us in the past day won't make up for what you did over the past couple of years, which of course ended with you killing me. I won't be getting over that anytime soon."

Luke blinked, taken aback. "Yeah, that's completely reasonable. I was just going to give you my number in case you ever need me, but...look, you need to understand that I'm so sorry for everything that I did."

"I don't care," said Jack. At his side, Eva nodded in approval. When he was arguing with Cordy, Lily, and Alix at the old house, he had thought that she was on the same side as the three others. He was grateful to have their strategist agree with him.

"I should get back." Luke started toward the fire-escape ladder and hesitated. He turned back around. "Just don't forget that I saved your ass."

Jack smiled. "I won't."

Grey eyes glinting in satisfaction, Luke extended his right hand. "Good."

They shook hands, and the Hunter left, zipping off in a blur. Jack stared after him, the man who seemed so desperate to gain his trust. Perhaps one day he would earn it, but Jack needed time. Now that the Dusk Walkers had their peace, he had all the time that he needed.

"There are too many cops on the road," Eva said to Cordy. They scurried around the rooftop, searching for ways to leave. "I guess we'll go along the train tracks."

She pointed at the termination of the dead end, where past the fence lay tracks that were covered in grass. They had obviously not been used in years.

They all agreed, and Lily took on the shape of a giant black bird. Alix hopped onto her back, and the two girls disappeared over the edge of the building. The bird returned for Cordy, and Jack went to stand in front of Eva. "I believe we have a date."

She stared at him, surprised that he remembered. "Yeah, we do. You gonna go all covered in blood?"

"Does it bother you?"

"No."

"Then it's settled." Jack took her hand in his, and they walked toward the edge of the rooftop, completely trusting their winged companion as they leapt off the building together.

END OF BOOK ONE

ABOUT THE AUTHOR

Zoe Quinn Shaw was born in Bloomington, Illinois and grew up adoring novels and superheroes. When she was twelve years old, she decided to combine her two passions in her first novel: *Dusk Walking*. She lives in Montreal with her parents, sister, and their dog Indigo.